Deck –
Hope you
the working's
, friends

SOME RAIN MUST FALL

Quigley
aka
Jack: Money

SOME RAIN MUST FALL

Jan Queley

iUniverse, Inc.
New York Lincoln Shanghai

Some Rain Must Fall

iUniverse, Inc.

For information address:
iUniverse, Inc.
2021 Pine Lake Road, Suite 100
Lincoln, NE 68512
www.iuniverse.com

ISBN: 0-595-26947-8

Printed in the United States of America

This book is dedicated to my husband, John, who has shown me what the words love and commitment really mean.

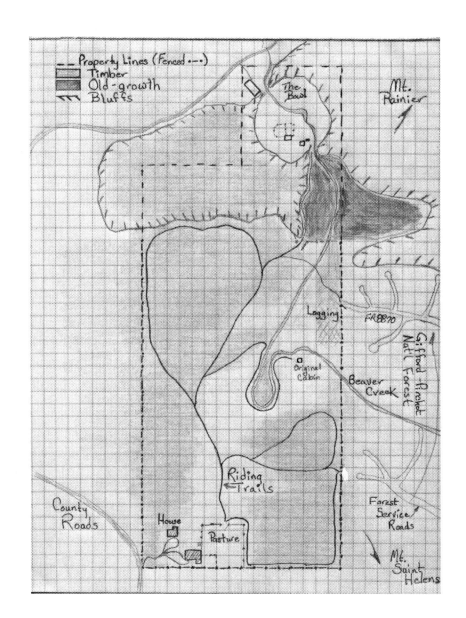

Property Lines (Fenced ·—·)
Timber
Old-growth
Bluffs

The Bowl

Mt. Rainier

Logging

FR 8870

Gifford-Pinchot Nat'l Forest

Original Cabin

Beaver Creek

Riding Trails

County Roads

House

Pasture

Forest Service Roads

Mt. Saint Helens

Into each life some rain must fall.

—Henry Wadsworth Longfellow

CHAPTER 1

Ben Mason dreaded the next few months.

"I'd do almost anything for Em. She knows it and pushes me. One day, Bronc, she'll shove me past my limit."

"Yah, right! You're a big talker, but I'll believe it when I see it. You'll take whatever she dishes out to you and smile." Bronco chuckled.

Ben let his thoughts range back over the past few weeks. Em had a hold of a bone and in her own way she planned to chew it down as far as she could. As usual, when she took on a new passion, she sought company. He smiled when he realized how she had pulled him into her current obsession. She believed they needed to be ready for her long awaited visitor. Her niece, Ann, was driving out from Chicago to see the Longley homestead for the first time and Emily wanted everything to be perfect for her.

"O.K. I'll admit I won't say no to her, but I don't have to give in totally. Em expects me to baby-sit this woman and she sounds like just the kind I hate, college educated goody two shoes. A pain in the ass. I don't plan to do much talking to her. I'll not say one word more than I have to. If I do I'll just get in hot water with Em. Easier if I just clam up."

"Maybe, but somehow I don't think that'll keep you clean either."

I'm finally here, thought Ann Harris with relief. It had been a long drive but she was thankful for the early June timing. Any later in the season and the heat of the drive would have been unbearable across the Dakotas without the air conditioning blasting. She was fulfilling a life long dream coming to the place her Uncle Henry and Aunt Emily called The Homestead. M bar M, however, was the sign Aunt Emily told her to watch for. The sign looked old, with the words burned into a weathered wood plank. It hung from heavy chain off an arch made of huge logs that spanned the drive. To each side of the gateway, a wooden fence extended about twenty feet to the woods, then changed to barbed wire.

Although too early for blooms, it appeared that the climbing roses on the fence would be spectacular later in the season. For now, there were a few late blossoming daffodils and a profusion of carefully tended primroses. To Ann the display felt like a personal welcome. It also demonstrated her aunt's continuing love for this place. Just as beautiful were the wild flowers popping up in uncontrolled abundance. There were little yellow violets and a soft lavender variety with dainty foliage that she recognized as a kind of bleeding heart. Ann drove through the gates and up the long driveway, where massive overhanging big leaf maples near the entrance gave way to evergreen trees as large as any she had ever seen. The trees grew close to the sides of the drive, their branches spreading to completely enclose the roadway in an umbrella of greenery.

At the top of the quarter mile drive, there was a road off to the right that led down to a large barn and several other outbuildings. They looked quite old but well cared for, but it was the house that drew her attention. It could have been off the set of an old Western movie. It was built of logs about a foot through. It's aged but impressive mass was softened with a wide verandah and porch swing. The only modern touches were the large picture windows in the front, which had been blended into the home's styling with wide wooden frames and sills. Peeking out of the right side of the roof was a large dormer.

Ann climbed out of her car and walked to the porch. Before she could knock, Emily opened the door. "Oh, Ann, I'm so glad you're here," she burst out with a rush, accompanied by a big hug. "I hate to leave you but I have an important meeting with my attorney. I shouldn't be more than a few hours. You'll be using the loft bedroom. There's tons of food, so help yourself if you need a snack. I should be back in plenty of time for dinner but I planned out a menu that's on the fridge. If that doesn't sound good we'll change it. Linen is in the hall closet. Bathroom is over there, but just explore all you want. Make yourself totally at home. There is no TV, but lots of books. Got to run." Another hug and she was gone.

Ann realized she hadn't even said Hello. Aunt Emily hadn't slowed a bit in the years since she had last seen her. She was the same boisterous, energetic woman she had always been! Shaking her head, Ann went out to her car to begin unloading her bags. With her arms full she headed where Emily had indicated the loft to be. Looking at the steep stairs leading to the second floor, she put down a couple of bags leaving one hand free for the handrail. She regretted, for the first time, the size of her wardrobe.

The loft room had all the charm you could imagine. The antiques fit perfectly with her idea of a well-appointed early ranch house. She wondered how they had maneuvered the large pieces of furniture up the narrow stairs. Then she noticed the pulley and pivoting arm hanging from the main beam, or more correctly, huge log supporting the open ceiling. Maybe the furniture had been pulled up and swung over the balcony rail. There was a massive bed with a delicately carved headboard. The night stands on each side held old kerosene lamps, but the one on the near side had been converted to electricity. She walked from one piece to another admiring their workmanship and style; a lovely old washstand with a pitcher and bowl, a wardrobe for her clothes, a matching highboy dresser and the most exquisite dressing table a woman could imagine. She couldn't resist sitting down, opening one of her bags and beginning to put some of her things onto the little shelves and into the drawers. No matter what else happened, this room was definitely going to have a special place in her heart for a long time. She already felt more like she was home than she had in the stark white rooms of her Chicago apartment. Well, at least, that apartment was behind her. She had boxed up or given away everything. When she went back she would finally buy the condominium she had planned for. This break from the rut she had gotten her life into would bring about many changes.

She got up and walked to the large dormer window. She could see the barn and horses grazing in a field nearby. From the small window at the back of the room she looked down on a neatly tended garden edged with flowers of every color. There was no front wall to the room, just a railing overlooking the living and dining areas. It gave the loft a marvelous, expansive feeling. There was an old dressing screen in case one worried about modesty in this open room, although no one could actually see into the room from downstairs.

The staircase was her only concern. It had sturdy wide steps and a handrail, but was quite steep. She was challenged to get the rest of her luggage upstairs, and by the end was exhausted. Still Ann began to unpack her things slowly and as she worked her energy bounced back. She hesitated over one bag not sure if she wanted her Chicago memories too close, but decided that was still an important part of her life. With that settled in her mind, Ann used a couple of nails in the logs to hang sketches of fashions she had designed.

When the loft room was fairly well organized, she set out to explore a little. Downstairs there was one large room that flowed from living to dining area to kitchen. Beyond the kitchen, a short hall led to the bathroom door on the left and bedroom on the right. At the end of the hall, a door opened onto a back porch with a little laundry room to one side. The backyard garden she had seen from upstairs had some flowers blooming already and more just beginning to bud.

She determined the next priority was a shower and came out feeling refreshed, but starved. A glance at her watch revealed the afternoon had flown by; it was nearly five. Well, she would start earning her keep right now.

Ann headed for the refrigerator. There was the menu, posted as Aunt Emily had said: green salad, rolls and Gramma's Casserole. She'd never made Gramma's casserole but the recipe was right there and she was feeling adventurous. She started through the refrigerator. There were no salad ingredients. Oh well, maybe Emily planned to bring them back from town. She went ahead with the casserole, finished it and popped it in the oven. Her thoughts strayed to how different life here would be than the bustle she was used to in the business world of Chicago. Here in this quiet setting she could imagine box socials, putting up jam and weeding the garden. GARDEN! She jerked herself up short. Of course, the garden out back had flowers around the outside but surely it was mostly vegetables. She laughed. She was such a city kid that this was the first time she would harvest her own vegetables for dinner. She loved the outdoors, but in Chicago that meant jogging, tennis and golf. Besides, the way she had been raised, there had certainly been no homegrown veggies. In fact, landscaping was something the groundskeeper handled.

She headed down the hall and saw a large basket by the back door. A few telltale, wilting leaves told Ann of its purpose. She took it along. There were carrots and peas still young this early in the year, but they would be sweet and tender. The cucumbers and tomatoes were just starting to flower but the radishes, green onions and lettuce were ready. Her thoughts and hands flew. How about some fresh flowers for the table? Those yellow ones are beautiful along with some delicate white ones.

She hurried back to the house with her basket overflowing. She hoped Emily was hungry, there was going to be plenty of salad. Setting all the vegetables aside, she went to the china hutch to look for a container for the flowers. Ann found not just a wonderful old vase, but also a whole collection of china and a set of silver. After arranging the bouquet, she went back to the hutch for a large antique bowl she'd noticed. This was like playing house with all the beautiful things one dreamed of. She found some polish and spruced up two place settings of sterling and some lovely old candlesticks. There was a special little piece for everything imaginable. She wondered if Emily kept these things just for show or if she really used them. They were so irresistible she couldn't imagine them just setting in a cabinet.

She finished her dinner preparations, made herself a cup of tea and sat down to admire her handiwork. The casserole had about ten minutes to go. She worried now that Emily would arrive to find it overcooked. Then Ann heard a car, it was her aunt's red blazer. Ann wondered if Emily always drove at such a breakneck speed. The Blazer headed toward the barn so Ann had a few minutes for the finishing touches of dinner. She was just ready to carry the casserole to the table when Ann heard Emily striding up the front stairs. Her aunt burst through the door. And she froze, staring at the table.

Ann had the sinking feeling that she had taken the invitation to "make yourself to home" a little too literally. "I didn't think you'd mind. Everything was so beautiful, I guess I just got carried away."

Emily only then seemed to realize that Ann was in the room. "Oh, my dear," she said, "it's beautiful. I just haven't used those things for over ten years, since your Uncle Henry died. It startled me, but those treasures are meant to be used and I've missed them terribly. You must be as starved as I am. Let's eat."

Emily was in a cheerful mood, chatting happily through dinner and drawing Ann out on various topics. "I hope everything is OK in your room," Emily said. "I wish sometimes I could use it myself, but I haven't been able to negotiate those stairs for years."

"It's the loveliest room I've ever had," Ann declared. "I spent a good part of the day up there just enjoying the great feeling it gave me. It's perfect and made me feel totally at home."

"Good. Ben will be pleased. Now tomorrow is errand day and it's always long and tiring. So let's get at the dishes and then off to bed. We talked so long it's already late. Besides, with all your driving and packing you must be exhausted." It was only after she was upstairs that Ann realized she'd not asked who Ben was.

Ben dropped by early the next morning, as was his habit, to share coffee with Em. "Well, how did it go," he asked.

"We talked for hours and I know we'll have a wonderful time while she's here. It's like we have always been together. I really hope she doesn't ever decide to go back there. Chicago is no place to live. I just hated it the couple of times I visited. I'm going to take her to meet a few folks today and if you have the lists ready I'll order the supplies and things."

"You know I always have lists," he said, pulling out a couple of slips. "If you expect her to learn to ride she's going to need some tough jeans, boots with a walking heel would be most practical, some flannel or tough cotton shirts, a hat with a wide brim and rain gear. I have a list for that, too. Now maybe she has this stuff but I doubt it from what you've told me."

Ann rose and began getting ready to go to town, which she assumed meant Morton. She had seen the name on the road signs as she drove in over the pass through the Cascade Mountains, but this would be her first sight of the town itself. She wasn't sure what this all day errands trip would entail but settled on a loosely flowing, buff linen pant suit and a rust silk blouse of her own design. It was one of her favorites and she liked the way it brought out the highlights in her hair. She styled her hair quickly in the French roll she preferred for her long, often hard to control, tresses. When she came into the kitchen, Emily gave her an approving nod and they chatted through a quick, light breakfast.

They drove about five miles before Ann saw the sign announcing "Morton: Heart of East Lewis County." Ann wasn't sure what she had expected, but this wasn't it. Morton didn't conjure up the term town in her mind, nor did it appear to be the heart of anything. She noted a logging supply and a secondhand store as they drove quickly through the downtown, all two blocks of it. Emily was spewing a steady stream of information: who owned each little shop, how long each family had been here, how many kids, historical data about the community. Morton has a population of 1280, Emily informed her. Ann guessed that that might equal the number of people in her apartment complex! She didn't have much time to absorb everything before they were at their first stop.

They made quick visits to three of Emily's friends, in what was apparently Ann's introduction to local society. Ann was delighted with each of these sweet old ladies. She also realized why they had eaten such a light breakfast as they were plied with homemade pastries at each stop. They finally made their way to a store where Emily ordered farm supplies and parts. She had a list neatly written out so the shopping portion of the stop was fast and left plenty of time to chat with the clerk. Emily assured him that Ben would be in to pick up the things she had requested. So, Ann thought, Ben is a hired hand.

"Well," asked Emily, "do you have anything you'd like to buy?"

"I can't think of a thing. I brought everything I'll need."

"Do you have riding boots, heavy jeans and shirts, a hat, and rain gear?"

"No. I don't. But I won't need them because I don't ride."

"As for rain gear, you're in Washington now, believe me; you need it. You didn't ride before, but you will. Ben will see to that. We'll just pop over to the Outlets and pick up what we need."

Emily's definition of 'pop over' turned out to be a 20-mile ride. Ann enjoyed the trip and was surprised at how quickly they arrived. There was almost no traffic and Emily pushed hard, loosely interpreting the speed limits of 60 and 70 m.p.h. Emily's Blazer was well named for the way she drove it. Ann despised Chicago's traffic jams. Around here traffic was a car ahead of you at a stop sign. The first traffic light they came across was at the end of their ride in a town called Centralia, right at the Outlet Mall. The excursion gave distance a completely different feeling. She lived only a half mile from her office in Chicago and it sometimes took longer than this to get there.

In the store Emily picked out a pair of boots she said had the right style of heel, a compromise for walking and riding. (Whatever that meant; Ann didn't ask.) Her aunt was busy talking to people in the shop and looking around for just the right things. Emily told Ann to pick any color or pattern of boot she liked with that heel. Ann pulled out her wallet but hesitated, still not convinced she would use any of these things. Emily reappeared, noticed her hesitation and seemed to read her mind.

"This is a welcome to The Homestead gift. You won't be the first visitor who has been outfitted here. You need these clothes to enjoy the place and I fully intend to see that you enjoy your stay."

"Aunt Emily, I can easily pay for anything I need."

"O.K. But there are a few more things."

Emily rushed off again and returned with a further selection of flannel shirts in different colors and patterns, as well as, some jeans. "If these don't feel good, there are lots of others. You try these on and I'll pick out some rain gear." Before they left the store, Emily had added a sturdy belt, boot socks and a black Flamenco styled hat with a wide flat brim and a string under the chin. Ann had really tried to talk Emily out of the hat and rain gear. She knew she'd never wear them. She hated the way hats mussed her hair and as for rain gear, you just stay in when it rains or carry an umbrella. Emily insisted and Ann finally gave in rather than hurt her feelings. Emily seemed so excited about their purchases; it touched Ann's heart.

They hurried back to Morton to meet a gentleman for lunch at a pretty little house converted to a restaurant. Hal Emerson was Emily's attorney and it was obvious that there was a deep affection between them. For the first time since she had arrived, Ann watched Emily quiet down to give Hal her full attention. They were so engrossed in each other; they only came down to earth occasionally to include Ann. It was fun to watch the two of them so plainly in love. It had never occurred to Ann that such a thing could happen so late in life. She had been brooding a little at being single in her 40's, thinking she was getting too old to find romance.

Hal reminded Emily of the meeting and luncheon the next day with his old law partners. She assured him she would be there. Ann saw Emily's quick glance in her direction. "Tomorrow," Ann said, "I'm looking forward to spending the day seeing some of The Home-stead. Don't worry about me."

Ben was in the barn when Bronco dropped by. "Well? What's she like?"

"I don't know," said Ben. "Tomorrow's the day. Em is going to do something with Hal. I'm supposed to keep Ann busy all day. How much do you know about multiple sclerosis?"

"Nothin."

"Me either, until Em started in on me. You know how she is when she's on a mission, best to get out of the way! She lit into this M.S. thing like she was planning a military assault. She's been researching without let up, and whatever she finds I'm was expected to study, too. The reading assignments were O.K., but the Support Group meeting she sweet-talked me into driving her fifty miles to attend was something else. I could see why these people needed support. Only about a half of them showed no visible signs of the disease. I found out some of them were recently diagnosed and a couple were truly lucky to have had the disease for years with only minor symptoms. The others were using canes, braces or wheelchairs. Ann can't be hit too hard yet or she wouldn't have driven herself this far. Still I don't think these next few months will make the list of my favorite memories. I've been putting off meeting her. I don't want to do it in front of Em. I figure Em will spot how antsy I feel about this and I don't want her on my back. Everything I've read about M.S. tells me Ann can do as much as she's willing to try, but a city girl like her, I doubt that will be much. I think this whole visit will be a bomb."

Next morning over coffee, Em updated Ben on the previous day's events. He made sure to arrive early each morning to help Em fill that part of her day. She had confided once that it was the time of day that she missed Henry the most. Henry and she had some of their best conversations those minutes before he went off to work, sharing the little things that brought them joy or concern in life. Ben knew he could only partly fill the hole left by Henry, but he fully intended to do his best, and he enjoyed being with Em. Since Ben was a kid, Em and Henry had been as dear to him as his Mom or Grandparents. Some people might not consider them closely related but in this small family every relative counted. Besides, Henry was every bit the father he had never known and whom his mother wouldn't discuss. Henry had gotten him out of the city he hated and set him on the right path. Now most all of his kin were gone and Em had his full devotion.

This morning Em's attention was on Ann, just as it had been the past few weeks. Ann was the only child of Henry's sister. Em and Ann had written and talked quite often, but hadn't seen each other in about ten years. Em was ecstatic about the visit she had proposed to Ann for a long time. Ben's role, he was told, was to teach Ann to ride and do anything he could to make her feel at home.

Em sparkled with delight as she brought Ben up to date on yesterday's activities. She always reveled in life and it was fun just hearing her talk about the little things that kept her enthusiastic about each day.

Today, as usual, Ben best liked hearing about anything that involved Hal. Em became so animated. She was like the old Em, the one he had known before Henry died. He wondered if Em knew she was in love again. He didn't think so. Hal had been a close family friend for so long, Ben didn't think she had sensed the change in their relationship the past few years. Em was excited. It was obvious she was looking forward to her day.

Now came the instructive phase of her dialogue. Em was looking him hard in the eye waiting, as always, to be sure he was really listening. She knew him so well. He often would drift off planning some project, or let his mind create a list of things that needed to be done. Today he was thinking about her and Hal, but she still sensed his mind wandering all right. When she was convinced she had his full attention Em told him she would be gone for the day and was relying on him to show Ann around and make her feel welcome. "I will Em. Does she have everything she needs to ride? That's the best way to get a feel for this place." Besides, he thought, it cuts the need for small talk. I can pick a narrow trail so we have to go one in front of the other. It would force her to quiet down and look around. A need for constant talking was always a problem with city people. Then he heard Ann coming down from the loft took a last gulp of coffee and ducked out over Em's objection.

When Ann came into the kitchen her aunt was alone. Emily told her she had already talked with Ben about showing her around. Emily looked over the outfit Ann was wearing, light blue slacks and a stunning floral blouse in muted tones of blues and lavender. "Ben", she stated positively, "has a low opinion of fancy clothes around the place. Be sure to wear all the things we purchased yesterday or he will be very hard to get along with."

After her aunt left Ann went to the loft to change, but she was irritated. How could Emily give in like that to her hired hand? He should be respectful of Emily's guests, no matter what they wore. Still, Ann wanted to please her aunt, so she put on the heavy, fairly tight blue jeans and cowboy boots. She selected a flannel shirt with a bright blue and green plaid that coordinated well. She decided the clothes weren't too bad looking, if you liked this style of dress. Except for the hat! She had just done her hair and the hat would just mess it up. Besides, she had never liked the look or feel of a hat. Ben would just need to get along without it.

CHAPTER 2

Ben released a young filly into the pasture. This was the only horse that needed to be kept in a stall. He talked at some length to owners before he agreed to take on their training. He felt it was important understand how they would care for their animal. If the horse would be regularly pastured, he pastured them at M Bar M. If they would be stabled, then that's the way they were handled here too. His own preference was to let them run free. It never got cold enough in the Northwest to be a problem. They just needed trees available for shelter from the rain and lots of pasture. For that reason he never accepted more than three or four animals to train at a time. Right now he had four young horses, plus his mare, Peanut, and an experienced gelding, Comanche, in the pasture. Comanche was a horse he picked up for Ann to ride.

Em told him he worried over things too much, not that she had any room to criticize on that topic. No matter. He was sure it was a mistake to ask someone with M. S. to negotiate the loft stairs. Em said Ann's symptoms were fairly mild so far and it should be all right. She felt Ann should make the decision whether there was a problem. It was worth some effort to stay in the loft room, he had enjoyed it as a youngster and he knew Em really wanted Ann to have the experience, too. Still he was not convinced that it was a good idea to have her up there and he planned to keep an eye on that situation.

His other reservation about this woman came from Em's regular bragging sessions about her niece's career. "She's an example of what a modern woman can accomplish," Em said. "Ann made her way from the bottom to corporate executive. She's a woman who knows what she is capable of and isn't afraid to go after it." That spelled trouble to Ben. She was probably near six foot, like other women he had known in Henry's family. They tended to rule the roost and could easily be overbearing and bossy. He was sure she'd take riding instructions like a stubborn mule. In his experience, these so-called modern women were extremely headstrong and needed to have their own way to make it clear to everyone why they were at the top. Besides, he'd tried bringing a city girl here once before. Angie had been a disaster. "I can hardly wait," he grumbled to himself, "to give Ann her first real introduction to the place." Keep saying it, he thought, you might start to believe it. Ben slammed the shovel into another horse pile. His wheelbarrow filled quickly.

Before she went down to the barn to find Ben, Ann wanted to look around a little on her own. She headed toward the lush, stump-littered pasture where several horses grazed. The animals were generally in the same section of the field, but scattered about in a relaxed fashion. Though they raised their heads slightly when she approached it looked as if they were going to ignore her. Two other horses were outside the pasture fence but stayed close seeming to enjoy the company of the enclosed little herd. One horse drew Ann's attention. She was strikingly different, smaller and stockier than the others, with a rebellious looking white nose patch that extended around her eyes. Her body was a vibrant red brown, except for some white patches that spread up from her belly. Her mane, tail and one foot were black. The other three feet were white making it appear she was wearing mismatched socks. Overall she had a wild, untamed look that was very appealing. The long legged, solid colored animals were more like what she had seen at the racetrack. They were regal, but seemed plain by comparison. To Ann's disappointment, her favorite immediately moved away and broke into a run, which stirred up the other horses. It was beautiful to watch. As the six kicked up their heels and raced away down the field, they seemed like many more and the thunder of their hooves carried clearly back to her. The stocky little rebel, even though she looked strong, wasn't able to keep up and was soon running last. Suddenly she turned and raced back across the field, straight toward Ann. She came to a sliding stop and reached out her nose. Ann was startled, but thrilled, and petted her. The horse wasn't satisfied with that and kept sniffing closer.

Ben had seen Comanche start his trademark game to lure the herd away. So Ann must be out there. He tugged his belt up a notch, his way of girding his sword. He moved over to his lunch bag, pulled out the apple he brought each day and left the barn. He stopped short when he saw the woman at the pasture fence. She certainly was nothing like what he had expected. Judging in relation to the horse's back she was about 5'5". Her hair was a beautiful auburn and tucked up in a fancy do. She was well shaped and the clothes she was wearing showed every inch of it. His heart did an irksome little flip, which gave him pause. The last thing he needed was to be attracted to this particular female. No doubt she was accustomed to that probably employed it to get to the top in the business world. If she had a hint that he was interested she would try to leverage it to get the upper hand. No way that would happen. He knew just the way to make sure this executive kept her distance. He was off to a good start by letting his beard grow for the last several days. He must have had a sixth sense about this whole thing.

She didn't notice his approach. All city, he thought, oblivious to her surroundings. He watched Comanche push aside her attempts to pet him.

"Looking for an apple," a soft, deeply resonant voice said. Ann whirled around at the unexpected comment. The man she faced was dressed in well-worn denims and a hickory shirt. He hadn't shaved in a while. Although he stood about four feet away, she felt as if he'd run his hand over her instead of just his eyes. She was irritated. She was careful with the way she dressed at work. Stylish but not advertising what wasn't available, that was the way she thought of it. Now Ann was self-conscious in the form fitting jeans. She suddenly wished she hadn't tucked in and belted the flannel shirt. It emphasized her bust line more than she would have liked at this moment. The stranger didn't seem to notice her discomfort, he just drew a knife out of a sheath on his belt and started cutting up an apple. He walked over and handed her the pieces. Their hands touched and Ann shivered. What is the matter with me, she thought. She turned quickly to break the spell and timidly held out a piece of apple to the eagerly waiting horse.

Ben liked the feeling as their hands touched, but noticed Ann's shudder. Besides the beginnings of his beard, he was wearing some pretty junky clothes. He'd been fighting this meeting as he slung on his duds this morning. Em hadn't said a word about his little rebellion, although Ben was sure she'd noticed. Well, he thought, I got what I wanted she's repulsed by the dirty ranch hand.

Ann was using two fingers to timidly hold the apple slice. Ben brusquely grasped her wrist and pulled it back. He straightened her fingers and laid an apple piece on the flat of her hand. "You'll lose a finger," he told her, covering the appeal of touching her hands again with a gruff voice.

Ann looked him over covertly. He stood about 5' 11". His lean but muscular body was evident even through his loose fitting shirt. He couldn't be described as handsome. His nose looked like it had been broken at least once and there was a small scar on his left cheek. His hair had once been jet black but had a splash of gray now at the temples and his eyes were a brilliant gray green. He looked calm at the moment, but capable of fiery anger. He was far from the Greek God sort popular in her old world; the kind, like Ed, that she was normally attracted to. He was more of a Sam Elliot with an unexpected magnetism and an unforgettable voice. She certainly wasn't interested in her aunt's farm hand, but wished he didn't have this effect on her.

Ben looked straight ahead as he noted her studying him. He wasn't self-conscious about that. He knew that despite his age he cut a good figure. He had no trouble attracting women, but generally didn't bother. He had only found two kinds. Either they were after his money or they were just in it for the fun. He hadn't found anyone who was interested in a busted up, recovering alcoholic horse trainer, just for himself. Well, there might have been one; but he had his dreams, too, even if he had set them aside for a few years. The woman for him would have to be capable, have some goals of her own; spirit was the way he thought of it. So these last few years he had given up on settling down and just focused on making a good life here, taking care of Em.

Ben's fist was clenching and unclenching. Ann couldn't help but note the action caused a ripple of well-formed muscles up his arm. She pulled her thoughts away from that. The nervous habit probably indicated that he wasn't happy to be assigned by Emily as tourist guide for the day. Well, if he worked as a hired hand, he needed to learn to do what his employer wanted. At least she assumed this was Ben, although he hadn't introduced himself.

"What's her name," she asked to get things back to more neutral ground.

"Who's?"

"The horse."

"Gelded but still a he," he said, barely concealing his laugh. He gestured downward. The horse's male gender was suddenly VERY apparent as he relieved himself.

Only a city girl could miss that, he thought as he enjoyed watching Ann color. Letting her off the hook, he went on, "Name's Comanche and he's smart enough to be one, too. Pulls that trick every day." He sensed her question and continued. "Runs down field and the other horses follow like sheep. He drops behind and lets them race on, proud of themselves for winning. Then he races back for a treat. Comanche just doesn't like to share. The others never catch on."

Ann gave that a moment's thought. It was a little hard to believe that a horse could be that clever and calculating. She didn't argue the point, just changed the subject. "We really haven't introduced ourselves. I'm Ann Harris. You must be Ben," she said as she put out her hand.

"Yah. Let's saddle up." He said, thinking, "Don't start that executive handshake junk with me lady". "I'll show you around the place. Didn't Em get you a hat?"

"Well, yes," Ann stammered. She was offended he hadn't acknowledged the introduction or her out-thrust hand. It was also irritating that he apparently knew of Emily's concern that guests measure up to his dress code. She was irked that he addressed his employer as "Em". It was disrespectful and Ann doubted he had the nerve to do so to Emily's face. The flood of thoughts left her speechless for a moment.

Ben filled the void. "Good. Go back and get the hat. I'll get the tack."

"No!" Ann's momentary lapse into thought was broken by her indignation. He was assuming that she would take his wishes as absolute. In her business life she had fought hard to get above being told what to do, frequently, by men without her skills or ability. Obviously, this hired hand had Aunt Emily bending to his whim but not Ann. No one told her how to dress.

Ben paused to look at her. He seemed to consider making a comment but then shrugged and walked on. His voice drifted back over his shoulder tinged with sarcasm, "Yes. Ma'am."

Comanche kept pace with Ben on the far side of the fence. Ann decided to follow too, as Ben was apparently not going to press his order. I guess he sees I can't be pushed, she thought.

Ben let Comanche into the barn and proceeded to give a running commentary on the saddling process in his terse style. "Saddle blanket protects a horse from the rubbing of the leather. Make sure the front cinch is plenty tight or it'll slide 'round when you mount. Back cinch hangs pretty loose, it just holds the saddle in place coming down a slope. The tie down keeps a horse from tossing its head which can easily break your nose." Then he paused and looked at her closely. "Comanche is a special horse, and he's yours to ride while you're here. But there are rules for safety: yours and his. Never let anyone else ride him. Always use this bridle, no other. Never underestimate Comanche's smarts; he'll take care of you, if you let him."

With that, Ben whistled and the big golden brown horse came over to be saddled. It's back was 4–5 inches higher than Comanche. The animal had a touch of black on its nose. Its mane was cut very short; roached she thought they called it. The mane, tail and stockings were a shimmering black. Ben immediately began to talk to the horse and rub her gently as he saddled her. The horse was a mare; Ann made sure this time

"What's her name?" she asked. The man seemed more comfortable talking with the horse than with her.

"Peanut." Ben said and finished saddling quickly. He mounted, looked over at her and said, "left side".

Maybe, Ann thought, she should tell him she couldn't ride, but he knew that or he wouldn't have explained so much. He just expected her to get up and she didn't want to let him see that she was nervous. She might lose whatever respect she'd gained in standing her ground about the hat. So she mounted from the left side, as instructed, a little clumsy but by herself. If this guy was waiting for her to ask for help, he would wait a long time.

They headed out across the pasture. Ann watched Ben, copied the way he sat and held the reins loosely the way he did. He glanced over and gave her a nod and that damned crooked smile. He obviously had seen her watching and trying several holds on the reins to get it right. She felt a little thrill at receiving his endorsement and perversely that made her angry. She shouldn't care if he approved.

At the end of the field he got down, opened the gate and signaled her through. "Close every gate, even if you don't see stock," he said. "There aren't many cattle, but they roam free."

Her immediate thought was, "Doesn't he ever converse, except to give out rules and orders?" She kept the thought to herself. Despite his attitude, he was her guide and Ann wasn't going to give in to his moodiness. "Why aren't there many cattle? Isn't this a ranch?"

"No." Ben was silent long enough to make Ann wonder if that was all the answer she would get. Finally he went on, "That's probably one reason why Em calls it The Homestead. M Bar M is our brand but it's not used all that much. Mostly raise timber. This is not good cattle country, too wet. With too many animals, it turns to a mud hole."

He pulled ahead on the narrow trail and left Ann to her own thoughts. They rode on and after a while she relaxed into the comfortable silence. When the trail widened again he slowed to let her come alongside. She studied him curiously as they rode. His eyes moved rapidly catching every inch of the landscape. He warned her with a casual flip of the wrist of little dips in the trail, low branches or just something worth seeing. His nostrils flared at times—he drank in the smell of the country. He reveled in it.

She easily fell under the spell. There was a special closeness to nature up here on horseback, even more than a walk in the woods. She had been on a backpacking trip once but this was different. Of course you covered a lot more country, with less effort, but there was something else. She just couldn't put her finger on what. Ben stopped and pointed to two deer feeding along the trail ahead. The animals didn't seem to notice there were humans nearby. She realized they must just see the horses and think the people were a part of them. That must be at least a part of the difference from walking; the wildlife was unafraid. It took two legs to signal danger.

Damn, Ben thought, she's scored a few points. She isn't gabbing like most fools do. Few people, who weren't raised in the woods, could stand a quiet stretch of more than a minute without turning on a stereo or just babbling about nothing. Silence seemed to make them nervous. He'd sure seen that with Angie. When they left the city, her personality had suddenly changed. She'd kept up a steady stream of loud jabber the whole time they were at The Homestead.

He'd been watching Ann's hold on the reins closely, too. That was his main concern with her and Comanche. Most green riders were very tense and jerked up at every little sound, but she was doing all right. She had carefully mimicked his style right off. Most surprising, she really appeared to like the place, but time would tell about that.

Tat! Tat! Tat! The rapid fire startled Ann and she spun her head toward the sound. She quickly spotted the flaming red head, just a few feet away. She beamed at Ben. She had no idea a woodpecker was that loud.

Later, Ben drew her attention to a large bird diving down for a kill. She looked at him questioningly. "Eagle," he mouthed. He seemed pleased that her question hadn't broken the unspoken code of silence. Later, she stopped to admire a cluster of wild flowers. They were a brilliant yellow and shaped somewhat like a short Calla lily. He broke into the first real smile she had seen. He seemed genuinely glad Ann was enjoying the beauty around her. She said she'd like to pick a few for Emily.

"Can, but I wouldn't." Still, he reached over and took her reins while she climbed down. As she approached the blooms, the ground squished under her feet, wet and swampy. She was mucking up her new boots, but decided it was worth it. She snapped off a large blossom and her senses screamed. The odor was strong enough to taste. She dropped the flower and jumped back almost falling in her rush.

"Pretty, but called Skunk Cabbage for a reason," he called out. She sheepishly abandoned her attempt at a bouquet and sloshed her way back to Comanche. Ben enjoyed teasing her, but envied her the childlike pleasure she showered on everything that drew her attention.

They continued on without a word, until they reached a brushy area. Ben pulled up and looked over at her with a little frown. "Stay here. I need to check a section of fence." He headed down a faint, overgrown trail. Peanut was a problem, jumping fences constantly. He had mentioned to Bronco that this section needed tightening, but wanted to know it was done before he let the mare out of the pasture. She was just stubborn enough to come right back here and last time she refused to jump back over. It took him three hours to ride her around to a gate. The darn horse loved to harass him that way.

This man is frustrating. She was doing fine with her riding, but he hadn't even asked if she would like to come along. What's more he had just assumed she would stay because he told her to. Besides, Comanche seemed a little restless just standing there without Peanut and he obviously wanted to follow. She admitted to herself that she was nervous, too. She'd never been this alone. She wasn't sure what all the sounds were. Some of them were birds but there was a lot of snapping and crackling, too.

She turned down the dim path. Quickly the brush closed in, but Comanche seemed to know where to go and she gave him his head. The limbs just cleared the horse's back. He didn't choose a route that allowed room for her. The branches were lashing her unmercifully. Ann's arms were somewhat protected by the flannel shirt, but to defend her face she leaned forward over the Comanche's neck.

Immediately he sped up to a fast walk. The branches were catching on her clothes and hair. She couldn't seem to slow him down bent over like that and couldn't sit up without getting hit in the face. Then she lost one rein. "Stop! Whoa!" This seemed to irritate him and certainly didn't slow him down. The final indignity was when a bough caught firmly in her perfect French roll. It pulled painfully and jerked her upright. She automatically pulled back on her remaining rein bringing the horse to a twisting stop and tying her firmly into the branches. It felt like her hair was coming out by the roots. The pain and frustration were too much and she felt tears welling up in her eyes. Comanche seemed anxious to keep moving but stood, nervously shifting his weight from side to side. Each twitch was torture to her strained scalp. She continued to chasten him, "Whoa!"

Ben seemed to ride up out of nowhere. "Easy boy." The horse immediately settled, responding to the calm voice. Ben looked at Ann trapped in her saddle and chuckled, he should have known she wouldn't stay put. "I can fix that hair problem," he pronounced, as he climbed down pulling his knife from its sheath.

Her near tears quickly changed to anger. "Stay back! Don't you dare cut my hair." She saw his eyes blaze with fire.

"Yes. Ma'am." Ben said with obvious acid in his voice. He stepped to Comanche's side, speaking quietly to him. Ann's eyes followed where Ben focused his now angry gaze and could see why the horse was tense. A sharp branch was pressed into the gelding's flesh. He was trying to back up to extricate himself, but couldn't do it without putting pressure on her hair. She saw no blood, but the needlelike point had to hurt and had gouged a strip of hair away from his beautiful red coat.

Ben kicked himself silently. This was his fault. He actually could have explained where he was going and how long he'd be gone. He could even have waited and checked with Bronco about the fence. Getting the horse tangled up like this was really his problem. Ben carefully pulled on the branch letting Comanche back away. The movement wrenched even more painfully on her hair, but Ann didn't complain. Ben looked at her for what seemed a long time then he stretched up and broke the branch holding her. He used the knife to cut loose a couple of the long leather strips that decorated the saddle. Then he reached out and pulled her off the horse. As she stepped from the stirrup, her legs didn't seem to work. She had stiffened up on their ride. She collapsed into his arms.

Ann immediately flushed as she was crushed to his chest. Her face reached just to the opening at the neck of his shirt and she found herself drinking in his scent. It was natural with a hint of hay, not cloying and sweet like most men's colognes. She could feel each of his fingers on her back. They seemed to be burning into her. Her lips were just inches from his neck, she started leaning toward him. Suddenly, a steel grip took each arm. Ben pushed her away from him and stood her roughly on her feet. He paused for a second, easing up slightly. When she steadied herself, he spun her around. Ben grasped her hair. This time she made no comment as he yanked the pins and debris from the remainder of the fancy twist. He stretched the strands back tightly and, less than gently tied it with the leather fringe—once at the base of her neck and again with a second piece near the end of her flowing locks. This left her hair tightly bound and hanging close to her neck. Ben pulled off his battered hat and plopped it on her head. "Mount up," was all he said.

Peanut had stood quietly through the entire goings on. Ben went back to her and mounted quickly, feeling the need keep moving. He had been tempted to hang on to the soft package that had fallen into his arms. She fit there perfectly. One more second of her hot breath on his neck and he'd have followed through on an almost overwhelming desire to test those lips. Pushing her away and turning her around should have calmed him down, but then he'd started on her hair. He'd been unnecessarily rough to keep from letting on how wonderful it felt to have his fingers in those rusty locks. Good thing his guilt broke the spell. Did he think he was 20? His drifting thoughts could have gotten her and the horse hurt. This had all turned out to be nothing, but enough was enough! As he rode past, he spoke to Comanche (the only one who had used his head in this mess) fondled his nose, and led the way out.

Ann noted that Ben didn't follow the low narrow trail. Instead of the path she had taken he moved Peanut slowly back and forth around trees, choosing the clearest route. She occasionally got into brushy areas, but by pulling the broad brimmed hat forward, her eyes and hair were protected. She could safely stay upright to guide her mount. By the time they reached the main trail, she felt pretty foolish. He'd tried to tell her a hat was necessary, but her pride got in the way. Then he'd tried to keep her out of the bushes. Why was she so stubborn? "I'm sorry," she told him, "I should have listened."

He raised one eyebrow, giving her a look that made her squirm. "Hats protect you from branches and sun. When you lean forward, your feet press back against horse's side, which means speed up. When you yell, a horse will often run from the sound. You're just lucky Comanche's used to yelling kids and ignored you. Many horses would have taken off and left you hanging from a tree by your hair. That isn't a riding path. It's a deer trail. Deer are a lot shorter than you are so they don't worry about low hanging stuff. That's your job." Lesson over, he turned for home, leaving her and her wounded pride to hurry along behind.

For the next week Ann and Emily worked around the house, tending the garden, and finding pleasure in their deepening relationship. They planned ahead, filling their days with canning and berry picking, making jam and other delectables. For a break from their chores, goodies in hand, they would visit one of Emily's friends or sometimes Hal. Ann made time almost every day to visit Comanche. She groomed him and practiced turns around stumps in the uncleared pasture. She also enjoyed watching Ben work with the young horses. She understood they had never been ridden and expected to see a bucking bronco display, but the most rebellion she witnessed was an occasional humped back.

Ben allocated time to his general maintenance work and training the horses. He was never short of horses to get in shape. Word got around when you were good at what you did. Before accepting a new animal, he found out who would use the horse, how old and experienced the rider was and what type of riding they liked. That way he knew how steady the horse should be. If the horse didn't have the right temperament for the targeted rider he would let the owner know and work out something to find them a better match. He had never found a bad horse, just horses mismatched with their owners. He was a firm believer in finding the right partnership between animal and rider, like he shared with Peanut. She was a real character. Most people thought he had named her for her color, but actually it was as much her personality as anything else that generated the name. After almost 20 years together, she was totally trustworthy but always a challenge. It was a great combination. She would stand and wait for him any length of time. But when it came to ditches and fences, you just couldn't tell when she would take a notion to jump. She was strong, too. Even with him on her back, she could clear a three-foot barrier from a standing start. More than once he had almost ended up on his can. Left on her own, even a slight sag in the fencing gave her free rein to roam. He enjoyed riding the young horses, but always gave Peanut plenty of attention. Soon she would go out to the Homestead range to gaze over the pasture fence with Henry's Blaze and Emily's M'selle, but for now, they could still enjoy a little time together.

That feeling of partnership was everything, he believed. That's what he'd always sought with a woman, too, but it had eluded him. He was torn in his opinion of Ann. He felt very drawn to her. He could see she was struggling, probably with the M. S., and it was wonderful how she seemed to shed that burden when they rode. He thought about trying to move their relationship to a new level, but didn't want to do anything to jeopardize what they had. There wasn't the slightest hint that she saw him as more than an occasional riding companion. Takes two, he reminded himself.

With the young horses he tried to develop trust and they generally came to him easily given time to overcome their natural caution. Slowly he would introduce them to the smell and then the feel of the blanket, halter, bridle and finally saddle. When he finally went up on their back, they appeared almost anxious to get on with it.

There was other work to do around the place, but he found himself focusing on riding more and more. It gave him a good excuse to spend time with Ann when she and Em weren't cooking something up together. He enjoyed those easy days showing her around his world. Maybe, he thought, if I just take it slow and easy with her something will happen to make her come around.

CHAPTER 3

Emily and Ann walked almost daily in the woods together. The first time they started the habit, Emily had asked Ann, "Do you remember that old poem about buying 'hyacinths to feed thy soul'?"

"Sure. Mom frequently recited it while she arranged flowers."

"Well, you can only get hyacinths in the spring. The land is here year round and always changing. It's walking here that feeds my soul. Besides my doctor thinks its great for my heart, too. From that beginning, they walked, sometimes just the two of them. At other times Hal would come out participate in their exercise.

Unlike the Mid-west, Ann learned the underbrush here was thick and frequently wet. Sword fern grew up in lush clumps that were beautiful but clumsy to walk over. Just as challenging were the Salal bushes. Back east Salal was something you paid florists for, but here it was practically a weed. She quickly learned the wisdom of skirting the thick fern clumps and Salal patches. An even better approach was to follow a deer path or wider trail made by domestic stock whenever she could. Ann was beginning to recognize many native flowers and other species. Emily was a fountain of knowledge on the varieties and uses of each plant. Ann was absorbing facts she had never dreamed of knowing or having an interest in. Young, green salmon-berry stems could be peeled and eaten; locals called it bear candy. When the Salal berries turned a deep purple-blue and hung in tempting clusters they were incredibly sour. Emily told her they could be made into a jelly but recommended against it since it takes about equal parts of berries and sugar. Plantain is used to take out the sting of a nettle. Boy! She had found out the hard way that nettles do sting. They looked so dainty, no thorns like Devil's Club, but the stings were very nasty. The burn lasted for hours. Too bad Emily and her plantain remedy hadn't been along that day.

The name, evergreen forest, had led Ann to expect a monotony of green but that wasn't the case at all. The forest was filled with an incredible mixture of shades and textures. The spruce had stiff sharp needles, almost a silver green. The cedar had pretty little cones and was a soft yellow-green. The firs were a deep emerald. Each type of tree had a unique bark. Emily could identify a variety by its bark, but Ann had trouble with that. The surface changed so from young trees to the old giants. There were leafy trees scattered around, too and Emily instructed her about them all. Cascara bark is used to make laxative by boiling it as a tea or you can sell the bark commercially. Alder is used for furniture or paper; cottonwood is fast growing, used for paper and there are several varieties of maple, some good for furniture.

While Ann could understand how someone from the open plains of the Mid-west could feel claustrophobic in these woods, she only felt wonder. More than that, she told Emily; she felt warmed, protected and comfortable. The surrounding branches just seemed to reach out and hug you. She was feeling the benefit to her soul too.

At Ben's suggestion Ann carried her rain gear behind the saddle or in a little waist pack if she walked very far from the house. When he said, "slip'em on at the first sign of rain," he wasn't kidding. She had doubted him in the beginning but soon found Washington lived up to its reputation for rain. From the first drop to a downpour took only a minute. When they took long walks Emily had a little waist pack to carry lunch and her protective clothing, too. She showed Ann that the thickly spreading branches of the big evergreens were good dressing rooms and that knowledge kept them dry more than once. The air was particularly crisp and fresh after a downpour. The rain encouraged new little mushrooms to sprout and softened the forest floor. The wet ground silenced her passage and allowed her to glimpse a couple of deer and closely approach a grouse. She was shocked but thrilled at the loud thrumming when the bird finally spotted her and flew.

She never knew what to expect. Sometimes Blaze and M'selle would pop suddenly out of the woods. Emily always had a little treat secreted away for them so they knew they were still 'oved.

Some days she and Emily just stayed close to home tending the garden and working around the house. Ann used to call this kind of work chores. But with Emily everything had a spark and was thoroughly enjoyable.

Each day was a new adventure and Ann jumped out of bed eagerly. No matter how early she rose, though, Emily was up first. She awakened to soft voices most mornings and assumed Ben was getting instructions for the day or keeping Emily informed about his work. A couple of times he was in the kitchen sharing coffee with her aunt when Ann came down but he quickly finished and left.

Ben found time on some days to take her out for a ride. Without his company she hadn't left the pasture on Comanche. Ann wasn't sure of the longer trails she and Emily hadn't walked. She found herself looking forward to her rides with Ben and his terse conversations. He usually took her beyond the ranch, out a back gate and up into the National Forest.

Ann carried her sketchpad and frequently added to the rough drawing collection she had started on her way west. So many of her experiences in the Washington were new to her, she wanted to have these first impressions preserved. The sketches were much more personal to her than a photograph and it was a real change from the clothing designs she had penciled in Chicago. She found it relaxing and it seemed natural in the serene setting of Homestead life. Ben never commented on her drawing or the time it took. He seemed totally content to rest against a tree while she drew.

Time with Ben allowed her to unwind from the busy days with Emily. Ann was pleased to have a companion who wasn't as driven as her energetic aunt and didn't expect to talk about anything personal. Her life was too confused right now. It was refreshing to just absorb herself in her new surroundings. She couldn't remember ever being with someone who seemed so content no matter what he was doing. Ann wished she could live that way. He had such a simple life, little money, no worries, no obligations, and no conflicts with the boss. She knew she would never be content that way but it was comforting to spend time with someone who could. It felt better than she ever would have imagined.

Ben found rides with Ann totally relaxing. He could keep his mind away from his lists of To-Do's. He kept their discussions to wood lore and horses. He was pleased with how quickly she absorbed what he shared and her obvious infatuation with the countryside. He loved to see Ann's eyes light up when he showed her someplace or something new. Her desire to capture each scene on paper spurred him to take her to more of his favorite places; little falls, great mountain views, and a hawk's nest. She loved them all. He couldn't help contrasting her reactions to Angie's.

He'd taken part in the parties and such at the University; what else was there to do in a city? He just assumed that Angie was killing time too. When he brought her home to propose marriage on the land where he hoped they'd spend their lives, he was stunned. She was frightened by the trees looming over her and told a little joke at dinner and didn't even notice that the punch line stabbed him to the heart. "I'll never live anywhere I can't see street lights every few feet." But that seemed a lifetime and several women ago. You'd think he could just leave it and move on.

When Ann thought back over their days she realized sometimes they had exchanged no more than a dozen words in their hours together. Still the communication was constant and she began to treasure their time together. They were slowly developing a special friendship.

Emily asked about the sketchpad one day and Ann explained, "The sketches are rough now. Someday I'll pick out my favorites to finish in charcoal." Emily surprised her, expressing delight with her own portrait and immediately recognizing the location of several of the scenes.

"I gave up riding about 10 years ago, too many aches and pains involved. M'selle was getting along in years and I put her out to pasture with Henry's Blaze. But I remember, like it was yesterday, some of the places you've sketched. I'd love to have one, if you don't mind."

"Pick out as many as you want and I'll finish them for you. I like charcoal better than water color or oils, is that O.K.?"

"Whatever you think. I love them now, so anything else you do will be fine."

Ann had fun completing the drawings. When they were ready she gave them to her aunt and was surprised to find them a short time later, framed, on the living room wall.

One morning Emily suggested they should ask some friends over. "Nothing too elaborate. I haven't entertained much the last few years, but I'm ready. What do you think?"

"Sounds like fun. When shall we do it?"

"Things are pretty informal around here. I'll just call and see who could make it Saturday."

'Who could make' it turned out to be the Caldwell's, who published a local newsletter; the Rausch's, who had a gift shop on the highway to Morton; a couple of Emily's lady friends, and, of course, Hal.

Saturday was warm and clear. The cool of the log house felt good. Emily and Ann served a casual buffet. Everyone was comfortable, as old friends learn to be. They spent their time in amicable debate about local politics and discussion of the Logger's Jubilee. Ann found herself drawn into a commitment to help serve at the Lion's Club Logger's Breakfast. They just assumed everyone in the community would want to help make the festival a success and surprisingly she found that she did.

After roving around the living area, Pam Rausch scolded Emily, "You've found a new artist. Are you keeping him a secret? You know I have to search for new items for the shop. So tell. Where did you get these?"

Everyone moved over to look at Ann's sketches. When Emily introduced the embarrassed artist, they all praised her work. Pam assured Ann she would be happy to display all the sketches she would part with in their gift shop. If she was interested, they could talk about the financial issues later. Bill Caldwell had another idea. If Ann would like some part time work while she was here, he could use some help adding interest to his advertiser's layouts. He could never afford either the time or the money for a commercial artist so his ads were very rough

Ann was overwhelmed. She sensed the guiding hand of her aunt in all this. She hadn't thought of her sketching as other than a casual pastime or a way to communicate her styling ideas. Now she could help out people in the community and maybe get a little pocket change without touching the savings she had earmarked to buy her condo.

When they were alone again, she hugged Emily and thanked her. Emily maintained doggedly all she had done was invite over a few friends. The rest was fate and Ann's talent. Ann had always liked and admired her energetic aunt but since her arrival the bond had grown considerably. Ann felt a trust she didn't think was possible.

Now she told Emily she was ready to talk about what brought her here so abruptly. "I told you about the diagnosis, but not the issues that came up as a result. What's happened to me recently has dredged up feelings I undoubtedly should have addressed a long time ago." Ann thought for a minute about where to start and decided on the beginning. Emily already knew the facts of her life and career, but they'd never talked about Ann's reaction to them.

"You remember when I started at the bottom. I wasn't quite twenty-two. Lorence Uniforms was certainly not the most glamorous area of the fashion world. But I was broke and happy to have a job. The business has really grown while I've been there. I'm not the only reason but I know I'm a big contributor. They recognize it, too, or I wouldn't have received the promotions I did."

Ann paused for a minute thinking about the work she had done to stretch the definition of uniforms. The traditional uniform market was police, fire, medical, and restaurant. The company had their long-term customers in those areas, but couldn't seem to break into new markets.

She was at a concert when the idea hit her. She developed the concept and began sales to professional choirs, orchestras and bands. Occasionally, she found a private school with funds to dress up their musical ensembles. This was a relatively conservative customer base. They didn't really want to think of their outfits as uniforms. As her sales grew, Lorence Uniforms dropped the second half of their name and promoted Ann to executive level. She was soon leading efforts to attract these and other exclusive and lucrative new clients. All her customers received custom designs; many ideas were sketched as she made her sales calls. Sometimes the meetings were face to face or she would send sketches of her proposed designs for further consideration. She adapted her ideas with the customers' direct feedback to exactly match their desires. At times, to complete a tough sale she would send the details specs back to Chicago, have a sample sewn and shipped to her prospect by air. The market had responded very well to her sales approach.

Ann reined in her thoughts and continued, "Leading the sales team called for me to do a lot of traveling. About three years ago, I began to notice that at times I would have an odd numb feeling in my side. I mentioned it to friends and they chided me for packing too many clothes. They said I was probably throwing my back out with heavy luggage. Several recommended a chiropractor. I didn't believe in Chiros, but after my doctor found nothing wrong, I decided to give it a try. Miraculously, after a month or so of weekly treatments the symptoms went away. So when about a year later I had a similar feeling in my leg, I returned. He fixed me up again. The next time, the numb feeling was in my face. I was scared. How could carrying a heavy bag do that? When I explained to the chiropractor what was happening, he sent me to a neurologist. A spinal tap revealed the M. S.

I said that couldn't be right or how did the Chiro make it go away. That's when I learned about relapsing, remitting M.S. The doctor said the episodes would come and go in a few months, with or without a chiropractor. He was very calming, telling me a lot of his patients have few attacks and little long-term impairment. There is no way to know if I'll be one though. He recommended I begin giving myself injections that's supposed to help with long-term results.

I didn't share any of this with people at the office. I didn't want any pity or need any accommodation. I'd been living with this before I knew what it was and couldn't see any reason to change. Even more, I wanted a little time to adjust. I wanted time to learn more about the disease, too.

About nine months later, I had another attack. This time it affected my balance. Oh. Maybe I should tell you a little about how I dressed at work. I tried to be stylish and yet dress for our customers' conservative tastes. I generally wore heels, mostly sling back. I liked to look a little dressed up. But now with my balance problem, I kept twisting my ankles. So, I changed to low wedgies and slowed my pace down a couple notches. I found little tricks that added stability like sliding a hand along a wall when walking down a hall. Occasionally I'd stumble a little but not if I kept my mind on walking. If I was talking about something serious that would take focus, I'd just stop moving. I didn't think anyone noticed.

In April, Ed Lorence, our CEO, scheduled his Spring Staff Conference. We always went to a resort for a week. Since my medicine needs to be kept chilled, I called ahead and asked to have refrigeration in my room. Ed's secretary, Corinne, is very possessive of each little piece of her job and is a terrible gossip. Her habit of dropping pieces of private information, accidentally of course, was the reason I handled the call myself.

At any rate, the day we were to leave, Corinne sent out a memo to everyone. I'm not sure whether she was in a snit because she found out I didn't involve her or if it was totally innocent, but the memo said: 'Special arrangements have been made: for Joe; smoking room, and for Ann; refrigerator for medicine.'

I felt trapped. Ed and I had been seeing each other outside work over the past year. We weren't openly dating and had agreed to take things very slowly to be sure that our relationship didn't negatively impact the business. Still, I felt I owed him an explanation.

I wasn't really ready to discuss my diagnosis, but I got Ed alone and told him. He made no comment but I could see it rocked him. I understood, I was on pins and needles, too. At the conference a few days later, he announced plans for several new account acquisition trips; but he assigned them to one of my staff. These were trips that I would normally have taken as a matter of course. He never said a word by way of explanation. I tried to catch him to discuss it at the conference and after. He was never free.

I was upset but I was sure everything would be O.K., if we talked it out. I didn't want to slow down. I wanted life to go on just as normally as possible. But Ed went on trips or Corinne would answer my calls and say he had someone with him. It became fairly obvious that he was avoiding me.

About a month later, Amy, (She's a friend in the Personnel Department) updated me on the recruiting she was doing at design schools. I was shocked, as these would be additions to my group and I knew nothing about them. I tried to hide my reaction and learned the request had come directly from Ed. He was in that day but totally booked up with conference calls, according to Corinne. I could see from her console though that no lines were lit, so I ignored her and barged in. Ed was there with his feet up on the desk. I asked him about the new hires."

Ann replayed the scene in her mind as she told Emily about it. The anger and pain of that day were as fresh as if they were happening as she talked.

"Ann," Ed began, "we have had excellent communications over the years. I know you will understand and respect my position, if I'm totally open with you. We're in a business where personal appearance is very important. It affects our ability to make sales. I didn't say anything about the changes in you when I thought they were temporary, you know, fixable by a visit to a chiropractor or something. But…Well, you know, they are just the first signs. You can only go down from here, and there is no way to know the time frames. I've decided to bring in some new talent to work under you, for the future of the business. You'll still be directing your group, but I think it will be easier on you if someone else makes all the sales calls."

"Ed, I don't want things to be easier. I want the work and the challenge. This is what I've devoted myself to. Many of our clients have worked with me for years now and there has certainly been no reduction in sales in the past few months."

"Not yet, but we both care about the business. I'm sure you see why I want you totally behind the scenes from now on. Then if your walk looks a little drunken, it won't matter. Don't worry. There will be no change in your salary, just a change in your work."

"This could certainly be construed as discrimination. It's an insidious kind; discrimination against a possible handicap." She had felt her temper flaring as the confrontation went on. Her career was done, reduced to a tiny piece of what she had worked for.

"Ann, calm down. This needs to stay between us, let's not have Corinne overhear. Besides, I know you would never resort to using the law against me; it's not your style. I've watched you deal with men over the years and we've talked about some of the things you've faced. You handle things yourself, without any legal interference. Anyway, I checked with my lawyer, just to be sure. This is just a basic reorganization that is within my discretion. You'll lose no income, so you have no grounds for a claim. You know," he laughed, "this conversation didn't even take place or at least you can't prove it did."

"I had no reply to that." Ann told Emily. "I was just crushed. He used things that we had discussed privately, as friends, and turned them on me. I walked out without a word.

That night I racked my brain for a sensible course to turn things around. Then I saw your letter and decided I would run away for the first time in my life."

"It's not really running away." Emily assured her. "This is a visit we've both wanted for a long time."

"I know but I decided to come now to give myself a chance to think and let Ed see how indispensable I am to his business. I think it will put me in a negotiating position. I thought just bringing up the trip would do the trick. I called Ed, at home, and asked for a four-month leave. He slammed me down again. He didn't hesitate. Just said, 'O.K. Without pay, of course, but I'll continue your medical and count your time away toward year end bonuses.'

He didn't even asked where I could be reached." Ann continued. "So I thought fine, since he didn't ask I'll make sure he can't find me. I'd been thinking about a condominium unit. The money's set aside, but I haven't taken the time to pick it out. So, I took you up on your offer and arranged to have the apartment rented to fill out my lease. What furniture I had, I sold and here I am. I haven't contacted anyone in the business since I left. I don't intend to for a while. Maybe that was a little childish, but my pride was hurt. I need to decide if I even want to go back or to move on to a fresh start."

"I'm not going to give you any advice on this. It's important you decide what you need. I know you'll do what's right for you. You know you're welcome here as long as you like. It seems to me that starting in a new direction might not be too hard for you, if that's what you decide. You have already settled one thing I agree with, not to sue this Ed. Someone should nail him for his attitude, it is against the law but…from what I know of M. S., stress is bad. He didn't fire you, so it would be hard proving discrimination in this case and whatever money you might win would not be worth the risk to your health. But whatever you do, you know you'll have my support"

"Thanks, Emily. It's helped just to have someone to talk to about all of this. It's come to me in the last few minutes that most of the hurt I'm feeling is that he could so easily set aside our relationship. I understand his fear. I have it too. But he didn't even acknowledge that, he just focused on business. I need to be more cynical I guess, look at the motives a little closer."

"Now dear, don't go painting everyone with the same brush!"

"Not everyone. Not you, Aunt Emily" She squeezed Emily's hand.

"That reminds me. You need to loosen up. Things are more casual here than the crowds you were raised with. For one thing, just call me Em, like everyone else does."

"All right, Em. So if we're going to relax and talk about just any-thing…when are you and Hal getting married?"

Em started in surprise and pulled her arms close to her chest in a clearly defensive posture. "Why do you ask that? We're far too old to think of that sort of thing. I'm 75, you know. We're just good friends."

"Aunt Em, I can't see that you're too old for much of anything. You have more energy than I do most of the time. You can't fool me with that we're only good friends line. I've seen you two together. Hasn't he asked you yet?"

"Well, he's certainly hinted around it. He knows though, that I'm pretty set in my ways. The Homestead is a big part of that. Hal probably wouldn't move out here because he's so active in the community. I think he loves living in town. Besides, what would happen to Ben if I left here?

"That's all flimflam. I'm sure Ben can take care of himself and you aren't stuck in your ways. As for Hal's activities, town is just not that far away and from what I've seen you're pretty involved in all that too. Living at The Homestead hasn't stopped you. I'm sure something could be worked out. Just look at the changes you've made to let me into your life here. Come on, what's really bothering you?"

Em paused for so long Ann thought she might not answer, but she waited her out. "The truth is, it's like using the old dishes. In some ways I'm still in mourning for Henry. I love my time with Hal but I miss Henry. I don't really think he would have wanted me to spend the rest of my life alone, but I'm not sure."

"I'll do you the same courtesy you did for me. No advice. But think, do you want to live the rest of you life alone? Just because you marry Hal, it doesn't mean you've stopped loving or missing Henry. You have something beautiful with Hal. Does he deserve to spend the rest of his life alone?"

"You have a point, dear, I'll give it some more thought. I have to admit I've come to look at many things differently these past couple months."

The next day Em said she'd like to go to town for a day with Hal. "Maybe," she said with a twinkle in her eye, "I won't be home til tomorrow." As they laughed together, Ann hugged her and assured her she'd do fine alone.

CHAPTER 4

Ann was excited about a full day to ride. She looked out the window and was thrilled to see the clouds, perpetually billowing in the sky here, were brilliant white. She was learning to discern the telltale tinges of gray that warned the wary to keep the rain gear close at hand. Today, however, showed none of those omens. It would be a day to get out and enjoy in the fresh air.

Ben was in the field, as he so often was. It was amazing to watch him draw the animals in. He seemed able to get any horse to accept him in a very short time. He had the same calming affect on them that he made her feel on their rides. Since arriving at The Homestead she had seen several people drop off or pick up horses. Em just shrugged it off as something Ben liked to do and suggested she talk to him about it, if she was interested. She had seen Em collecting money from the horse owners so it must work out well for the ranch but it did seem an odd arrangement. Ben spent a lot of time at it. Maybe she would have a chance to ask him about his pastime today. She laughed to herself. She might even luck out with more than a two-word response.

Ann put on her hat, having learned her lesson, but felt like celebrating the beautiful day with something other than jeans. She selected some casual loose weave slacks, a long sleeved, light knit shirt and her boots, of course. She hurried down and found Ben in the barn. He eyed her outfit, with a frown. Ann ignored that; she was not going to let his disapproval spoil her day. But, Ann was startled by his appearance. His shirt was soaked and clinging to him. His brow was dripping with sweat. She couldn't imagine what he had been doing. It just wasn't near that warm.

Before she even expressed her wishes for the day Ben cut her short, "I can't ride today. You go ahead."

Thoughts raced though Ann's mind one after another. She knew they weren't entirely rational but couldn't stop. She was looking forward to this day. She was Em's guest and he should accommodate her wishes. He was just doing this to punish her for not dressing according to his whims. She didn't want to expose her feelings, however, so she replied quickly and firmly. "I've never been out riding by myself and I'm, frankly, unsure of the trails."

His eyes seemed to pierce through her facade. "We're not running a dude ranch, there's work to do." He took her arm and pulled her around to see where he'd been working.

A large metal pan was filled with glowing charcoal; obviously it was raised to greater heat by the large bellows suspended above it. There were a number of horseshoes laid out near by.

"One of the fillies lost a shoe. It's fine because it's about time to do some trimming anyway. And, no, I don't want you to stay. The horses will just be harder to work with someone else here." He said, before she even offered.

He always seemed to able to look into her mind and it was irritating. Ann felt foolish and rebuffed. She knew she had been unreasonable, but she stomped out to find Comanche. As she saddled him she calmed down. Now that her plans were up in the air, the thought of heading out alone was kind of intriguing. If she stayed to the trails, it didn't seem as if she could have any problems. Besides she wouldn't give Ben the satisfaction of seeing her give up on her riding plans.

Ben watched Ann walk away, annoyed with himself. He needed to do some work but Ann could have stayed and learned a little about farriering. Then he could have gone riding for a few hours. He knew he had just reacted to cover his feelings. Ann had looked too good in her outfit, too glowing in her excitement. When she looked that way it sure didn't help his resolve to remain aloof. Besides, she set him on edge when she took him for granted. She assumed that he would be available to her whenever she fit him in her schedule, and he had to admit to himself that he had been for the past month or so. He enjoyed her company too much for his own good. So he'd taken his discomfort out on her, maybe to prove to himself he could say no. Well, there was nothing he could do about it now.

Ann rode across the pasture and out the first gate. She headed to an entrance into the Gifford Pinchot that she and Ben hadn't used since she had first arrived. She used the shallow river crossing as she had with Ben but then she ran into quite a mess. Many trees had been cut. There was some equipment standing in the now open area. She was very surprised. This must be part of Em's land and nothing had been mentioned about logging.

She decided she had better use a different trail and retraced her path. She soon began to really enjoy herself. The rides with Ben were pleasant and she learned a lot, but she was always aware of Ben nearby. She hadn't needed to find and follow the paths or even select the direction they rode. She felt very adventuresome out on her own. She knew it was illogical but felt a newfound empathy for early western explorers, finding their way though the wilderness without even the trails she was following.

She meandered slowly, thoroughly enjoying the sights and sounds around her. She was pleased to discover that she was over her initial trepidation at each unfamiliar sound in the woodlands. Little pieces of the slopes of Mt. Rainier would peek at her from time to time through the trees and wild the flowers were as enchanting as always.

She purposefully turned onto a trail she had never explored with Ben. After a while it came out at the river on a high bank. Ben said it wasn't a river, just a big creek. That might be true in the scale of the west, but where she came from it would qualify as a river. She could see that the trail she was following circled around a long winding bend in the flow. The peninsula sticking into the bend was high at this end and cut off any view of the far side. She nervously rode Comanche down the rocky winding trail to the water's edge where the path continued along the curving bank. She had followed the river for some distance beyond the little peninsula when she saw the remains of an old cabin. She rode near the ruins and used her saddle rope to tie Comanche firmly. She loosened the cinch and slipped the bridle as Ben had shown her, so the horse could graze comfortably while she explored.

There wasn't much left of the place. The logs of the cabin had disintegrated and the roof collapsed in the moist Northwest atmosphere. The most poignant reminder of these settlers was a seat carved into a cedar stump. The stump was large and the seat just sized cozily for two. Although the stump was very old, the seat showed signs of recent tending. She felt drawn toward this special spot, sat down and lifted her eyes to the view across the valley. Most of The Homestead had towering trees everywhere you looked, but from this spot the panorama was open to the Northeast. The setting was one of a kind. Sitting on the cedar chair she looked directly at Mount Rainier commanding the whole landscape as it towered above the surrounding hills. She felt as if she could just reach out and touch it. The sun shown on the sparkling snow-covered glaciers and she could see clearly dips and clefts in the white expanse. There were jutting formations that must indicate a buried base of jagged rock. Some rough places cast shadows that kept the surface from displaying a monotony of white. The shadows had beautiful blue shades. It was a sight worth the time to study. She retrieved her sketchpad and took her leisure preserving the details of the scene.

Her drive across the country had taken her through the Rockies. Their spectacular, rugged peaks towered everywhere but still she found the Cascades more impressive. Mount Rainier was the difference. As she drove across the flats of Eastern Washington, the foothills gave way to the mountains quickly, but the sight that held her attention was Rainier always far above the range. It loomed higher as she drove, eventually dominating the road ahead. When she had come in June the snow on the hills had a five o'clock shadow of green peeking out of the gleaming hillsides. Now the foothills surrounding the mountain showed a patchwork of lush green timber and the light green logged squares. They formed a crazy quilt on the landscape.

When her sketch was finished, she looked further to her right and saw a headstone with Forget-Me-Not's growing at its base. She walked nearer and read 'Martha Longley 1864 to 1888. A good wife and loving mother.' Younger than I am now when she died, Ann reflected. It must have been a hard life here, clearing and farming this land. The stone itself was obviously much newer than 1888 and the grave was carefully tended. Someone cared enough to see that this woman wasn't forgotten. She didn't understand how Martha fit into the Longley family. Another question for Em.

Ann continued to explore. Wandering down to the river, she removed her boots and waded idly. She had been surrounded by people all of her life. She lived by herself and frequently traveled alone but here she couldn't call out for help or ask someone directions. She couldn't remember ever being totally on her own before. Far from loneliness, she was incredibly free. She felt a growing confidence in herself and her ability to deal with all that life was throwing at her. Knowing that she was constantly confronting the unknown, successfully, in this land was powerfully uplifting. She had confidence, for the first time that she would grow back into the self-assured person she had been, before. She had a habit of using major points in her life to define her situation. Everything in her life, she now divided into before and after the diagnosis. Sitting here in the breathtaking surroundings, Ann knew that was the wrong way to split her life. She should think of her life as before and after coming to The Homestead. Here she was beginning to understand herself at a new depth.

She thought back to the devastating times she went through after the call in her sophomore year in college. For a very long time that call had been the key before and after point in her life. The police had told her she was needed at home; both her parents had died in a car accident. She and her parents enjoyed the high life, belonged to the best clubs, lived in the best neighborhoods. She attended a prestigious college that her parents felt appropriate for their standing in the community. She believed her family wealthy and gave no concern to the cost of her education or her life style.

The truth of her financial situation was almost as devastating as the loss of her parents. They were in debt to their ears. Ann learned that harsh fact even before the formal reading of the will, as the creditors besieged her. She sold her parents' home and other assets to pay off most of the debt. She hauled herself out of her spoiled childhood into responsible adulthood. She quit school, went to work to support herself, and although not legally obligated, little by little paid the remaining creditors.

Thinking back on it now, with the clarity of distance Ann realized that her decision to pay everyone off was not just because it seemed the honorable thing to do, although that's what she told anyone who asked. The sacrifices she had made to come up with the funds had given her relief from the knowledge that she had contributed to her parents' financial woes. They never gave her a hint of any need for restraint, but Ann felt she would have known if she'd been less focused on herself. She needed to be careful this time to really understand what was behind her actions. She had spent a lot of time building her career at Lorence and it would be ridiculous to just walk away on a whim or in a snit over perhaps imagined or exaggerated slights.

The only thing that kept her head above water in those first few years after her parents died was her talent. One of her professors, impressed with her creative and artistic abilities, helped her get the job with Lorence. The company was far from glamorous, but competition in any phase of fashion is fierce. Regardless, she held her own. No actually she had done better than that. She paid her debts, used night school to finish her degree and worked her way to the top. What's more, she moved the business in a new direction. She was the driving force behind almost doubling the firm's profitability over the last 17 years. She had pulled in groups playing the cultured circuit, focusing on those that were well and privately funded. Her fashions had been on stages around the world, from Carnegie Hall to Paris and Moscow. She had a right to be proud, but that wasn't what drove her.

An honest look into her soul told her she had driven herself, looking for security. She now wanted desperately to set that aside and just meet whatever came at her: head on. She had stayed at the job with Lorence despite some other attractive offers because she had thought it secure, but now it didn't feel that way. When she set the finances aside, she realized she was no longer getting satisfaction from the work itself. The challenge just wasn't there anymore.

Sitting in the shadow of the mountain, she was drawing some of its great strength. She made the decision not to go back to the Lorence Company or Chicago. She would stay permanently out west. She could find work in Seattle and stay close to her aunt. Em was the last of her family and becoming more precious to her every day.

She glanced at her watch. She had been gone nearly five hours already. Ben was probably worried. She would show him there was nothing to be concerned about. She tightened the cinch, slipped on Comanche's bridle and mounted. Starting home with a new feeling of determination, she decided she would head back via the straightest route instead of doing more exploring today. Comanche almost immediately broke into a trot, but she tensed. A horse that would run for the barn had been her greatest fear of riding. She had friends who took riding lessons and told of the terrors of this occurrence. She pulled back on the reins, harder than normal. Comanche stopped instantly, almost unseating her. He turned and looked at her with what looked like disgust. His look seemed to be chiding her "I thought you were excited to get home!" Ben said he was smart, maybe he did sense her mood. She started him out again and he stayed to a steady walk. Then, confident he would stop when she wanted, she leaned slightly forward and pressed her legs into his sides. He turned his head and eyed her closely. "You mean it this time?" He seemed to ask.

"Yes," she told him, "just take it gently." He did. At her urging he changed to a fast walk and then a trot. At first, she thought she would be pounded to pieces. Then the pounding seemed to ease. Ann was pleasantly surprised to find herself moving with his rhythm. As they approached the big bend in the river, Ann decided she would cut off a lot of time if she went straight through the river and over the peninsula. She hadn't been off trail much and thought she would enjoy the change. Besides the route as far as one could see, looked pretty clear. There didn't seem to be the heavy underbrush that abounded most everywhere. Maybe the river overflowed enough to keep it washed away here.

She turned Comanche down the bank. Crossing the river to the peninsula was easy. She got a kick from splashing through the shallow riverbed. Her feet stayed dry and the horse didn't seem to mind either. She found her way up and over the small knoll in the center of the peninsula without a problem. When she looked at the other side, however, she saw that her guess had been right. The water did wash up on to this knob at times. It might keep the brush down but it had also deposited quite a mess. A tangle of branches and fallen trees blocked her way to the water. She could go back, but that didn't fit in with her new resolve to drive forward. It would probably be best though if she walked ahead of the horse and made sure there was nothing for him to get caught in. She dismounted and set out. It was frustrating work but she was slowly finding a way through.

It all happened in an instant. Her loose weave pants caught on some brush and she went down. She was flat on her face with the reins in her hand. Her fall had pulled Comanche right over her back. She felt his hoof resting on her. Terrified, Ann held her breath, waiting for the crushing weight. It never came. After what seemed like an eternity she slid sideways and stood up. She was greeted with a nuzzle and a look that seemed to ask "You O.K.?" The horse loomed over her, balancing easily on three feet. She stood and hugged him. "Yes. I'm fine. Looks like you're steadier on your feet than I am, so if you don't mind I'll ride the rest of the way." She climbed up and gave Comanche his head. He picked his way carefully through to the water. Once in the swirling flow, she found it was deeper than she expected. She lifted her feet from the stirrups to keep her boots dry. When they reached the other side the bank was steep. They followed along the shore toward a spot it would be easier to climb. The left stirrup was twisted, she couldn't get her foot back in. As she leaned forward to turn it, Comanche stumbled in a hole. She went right over his head, flat on her back in the shallows, in six inches of mud and right on top of that infernal hat.

The breath was knocked out of her and she lost hold of the reins. Before she had time to worry about losing her horse, he nuzzled her. "Yes," she said, "I'm on the ground again. It's my fault not yours." Her voice seemed to calm him. He waited patiently as she attempted to wash off the mud. It was a lost cause, the soaking blouse and pants clung to her and she only succeeded in changing the mud to a slightly lighter shade. She finally just picked up her hat and put the soggy thing on her head. The precise, flat brim she had started out with now sagged badly to one side. So much for dry boots, fancy pants and blouse! Now she looked like she had lived here in the mud and rain forever. Since she had resolved to stay west, she might as well start being sensible about her clothes from here out. That's what this country demands, she thought. She led Comanche, slogging through the mud, to the sloughed bank, mounted and urged him forward.

She thought, as they rode, about the bond forming between her and the horse. "Who," she asked him, "would have ever believed I'd be riding along covered with mud and talking to a horse? I'm picking up Ben's habits!" She could feel the laugh from her toes through her whole being. She might be a mess but she couldn't remember when she'd felt this good. In real partnership they happily increased the pace. She even let him try a gallop for a short while. It felt all right but the trail was a little rough and she soon slowed him. His immediate response to her gentle tug on the reins built her trust even further.

After passing through the gate into the pasture, she decided to see what she was made of, as they said in the Westerns. She goaded Comanche on and he responded as if he too was ready. The horse moved in a few paces from a trot to a gallop to a run. It was exhilarating. She clung to the saddle horn for a few seconds and then, as she felt the rhythm, she went back to just the reins. Her hat flew off her head straining to fly away but held firmly by the string around her neck. She could feel the wind rushing through her loose ponytail, flapping her soaked clothing with a cadence that matched the horse's break neck pace. Everything was right with the world. Not understanding where it came from, she let out a long, loud, cowboy yell. She raced into the barnyard and pulled Comanche to a stop. Expertly controlled, she was positive! No one stepped out to greet her and she was relieved that she didn't need to explain her mud soaked condition. She glowed as she unsaddled, grained and groomed Comanche. She hummed to herself as she headed back to the house.

Ben had finished his blacksmithing. As he worked he contemplated going out to search for Ann. She had been gone a long time, but he really didn't feel she could get into any trouble, since she was a very timid rider. He was on the barn's second floor forking down hay, when a movement at the pasture gate caught his eye. She was back, so he returned to his work. When he heard her yell, he quickly stepped to the loft door to see what was happening. The woman who galloped with abandon across the field was not the one he knew. She was not tentative about her riding. Comanche was running full out. Surprisingly she wasn't frightened, she was urging him on! Her clothes clung to her like they were soaked, but that wasn't what made her different. She wasn't worrying about her looks or anything else. She had been in a fight with a lot of mud and water and had obviously lost but she didn't seem to care. Here was a woman he would like to get to know better. A lot better. He was certainly seeing more of her now, those wet clothes left little to the imagination. So much for his resolve to stay aloof. He was damn curious to know what had happened on her ride.

Now, however, he didn't want to dampen her personal moment or make her feel the need to explain her appearance. Besides, he needed time to think about what he was going to do, so he stayed where he was until she had gone to the house.

Ann was flying high, held aloft by the sheer joy born in the realization that she could and would make it on her own. She would have a good life despite her medical issues. Her confidence in herself was restored. She was whole for the first time in many months.

Her mood was raised even higher by life at The Homestead. Here everything was so basic. She was immersed in nature and the people of the community; not pavement, traffic and business. She was enjoying feeling needed and appreciated. She had agreed to go in on Thursdays and work up any ads that Bill Caldwell needed. He had a lot of ideas for potential advertisers and they were working their way through them. As for her charcoals, she had finished up a couple sketches for Pam. She didn't really expect a large demand, but Pam and her aunt were pleased by the idea. Neither effort would bring in any real income, but she enjoyed being involved with her neighbors.

She couldn't accept her aunt's hospitality much longer. She had set herself a limit of four months. By that time she would have to give a final answer to her Chicago employer. Although she told herself she had made up her mind, Ann was still clinging just slightly to her desire for security. She hoped to have work lined up in Seattle before she told Ed of her decision to quit. That gave her about six weeks to find something permanent.

In the meanwhile, she wanted to pull her full weight so she planned to take on more work around The Homestead. She had already taken over responsibilities around the house and sent Em off to spend more time with Hal. Em didn't take much coaxing and came back with great antidotes. Lots of laughter filled their evenings as Em shared her days or told colorful stories. It was like their roles were reversed, Ann feeling like the older sister listening to her aunt's tales of her fun times with Hal. It made Ann more aware of the lack of companionship in her life.

Ben never willingly told Ann about work that was needed on the place, but if she persisted, he would accept her help. He always had a list of things to do. At first he seemed unsure of her sincerity in wanting to learn, but once he saw she took her work seriously he seemed pleased with the assistance. The extra help seemed to speed up the work, too. On the other hand he seemed to be gone from The Homestead more frequently than when she first arrived. She had been alone at least two days a week. He offered no explanation and she didn't ask. It gave her time to keep up with her commitments. She had work around the house and spent a lot of time completing charcoal drawings and advertising proposals.

CHAPTER 5

One night after Em returned from town, she told Ann they would be having company for dinner the next evening. Em was obviously excited and wanted everything perfect. She started through the sideboard and other hideaways, finding old treasured pieces. Ann spent the next day polishing silver, picking vegetables, dusting, vacuuming and arranging bouquets to scatter around the house. Em was out in the kitchen, baking and preparing delicious smelling dishes for her special meal. She told Ann to set places for five.

They took time out only to shower and dress. Em showed Ann the floor length hostess gown she planned to wear. "It may be old," she said, "but it has lots of good memories."

The gown was a deep maroon. "It will bring color to your cheeks and contrast beautifully with your silver hair," Ann told her. "But I think this style dress deserves a little elegance to go with it. How about an upswept hair do?" Em liked the idea. Her hair wasn't very long but after diligent effort Ann got the effect she wanted.

Ann had only a few minutes left to get ready herself. As she hurried upstairs, she noticed that she was feeling some clumsiness in her walk. She had had a long day and must just be tired. She refused to believe she was starting an M. S. attack. She reminded herself to be careful on the ladder and held the rail firmly. Once upstairs she dressed quickly, choosing a very modest skirt and blouse, not wanting to intrude in any way on the stunning period affect her aunt would make. She didn't have time to do much with her hair, just brushed it out long.

From the loft she could hear Em open the door. "Em! Is that you? You're 30 years younger, just the beauty I remember. The place looks like the old days, too."

"Ann got out the china and silver the first night she was here. We've been using it often. You'd know if you came into the house for more than morning coffee."

"I can see she's a good influence on you, within coming around to mooch meals."

Ann recognized Ben's voice but couldn't believe he was talking in sentences more than three words long! She came down the stairs slowly. She hardly recognized him dressed in a beautifully tailored camel hair jacket and deep brown slacks. His shirt was worn comfortably open at the collar. What had been unshaven scruff when she arrived in June had filled out. Tonight he had given it some finishing touches and sported a neatly trimmed beard. While it was mostly black, she noted the striking silver streaks down each jaw line. She grudgingly admitted that it gave him a very appealing look, adding to his rugged strength.

As Ben watched Ann descend the stairs, he was aware of her caution. He felt a pang of guilt. Em had mentioned how much she liked the loft and he knew he should have come up with a safer way for her to get up there. Between worrying about the logging and spending so much time with Ann, he just hadn't figured out a final solution yet. He watched her speculatively, but his attempt to focus on planning was hopeless. He liked the simple outfit she had chosen. Somehow the soft neckline drew your eyes to her face. Not that he was tempted to look anywhere else in the room. She didn't need fancy clothes to be appealing to him.

A car pulled up the drive and Emily hurried out. Ben's gaze never left Ann. As she reached the living room floor she looked up and met his eyes. Ann knew he had been watching her come down. She was conscious of her tentative walk. She assumed from that speculative smile that he had noticed and wondered about it. Ann felt a flush developing. He always seemed able to bring one on. She acknowledged Ben with a nod but moved past him toward the door. Glancing back, she saw that his eyes followed her. If she didn't know better, she would think there was something more to his interest than curiosity about her clumsiness.

The last two guests turned out to be Hal and another man about Ann's age. He was introduced as Dalton Emerson, Hal's nephew. Dalton was about 6' 2", blond, tan, and strikingly handsome. Impeccably dressed, he had the 'in' look of Ann's Chicago crowd. His light brown suit said money and concern for the latest style. Em and Hal, after quick introductions, headed for the kitchen, talking quietly. Ann was left with the two men. They were obviously well acquainted and their animosity rode scarcely under the surface.

Dalton began introducing himself to Ann, explaining that he was an attorney. He had graduated from Yale and after a few years with a New York firm had decided to move back West, closer to his aging family. He had set up practice in Seattle. He addressed all of his conversation to Ann. She made several attempts to include Ben, but he didn't help. He just kept giving his standard one word replies and she soon gave up in frustration.

Ann was glad when Em announced that dinner was served. It was a comfortable and delicious meal. Em quickly pulled Ben out of his morose mood. The affection between them, much to Ann's surprise, was obvious. Em treated him more like a son than a hired hand. I suppose, she thought, it's natural as much as she has had to depend on him since Uncle Henry died.

Finally Em couldn't contain it any longer and announced that she and Hal were engaged. They had set the date for October 1. The wedding would be here at the house and they would have a reception in town. Everyone was thrilled for them and a lot of hugging and laughing followed.

"What about the honeymoon?" Asked Dalton.

"Trust you to think of that first!" Em chided.

"Now, Em, I didn't mean it that way. I just wondered if you'd planned one." Dalton blustered.

Hal laughed. "She can always get your goat. Of course we're planning one, just haven't settled on it yet. There are a number of places we want to go, so we just have to pick what will come up first. Our honeymoon will go on for a long time." The look he cast in Em's direction left no doubt he meant it. Em and Hal insisted on washing the dishes alone, saying hot water was good for their arthritis.

Soon the threesome was alone again. To keep the conversation moving, Ann started telling of her adventures. She made it quite exciting. Her first sight of real mountains on the trip west, learning to ride, almost getting stepped on, being thrown in the mud and running full out in the pasture. Ben thoroughly enjoyed the story. Dalton, however, was upset. "Sounds like you've been given too much horse with your lack of experience." And with a glare in his direction, "Ben is famous for that."

"I reserve that fun for you," Ben replied with a derisive laugh. Ann thought that might be an interesting story, but realized she'd better not ask if she wanted to keep the peace.

Ben let them babble on as he mentally relived the little scene Dalton referred to with some relish. He thought it had helped Dalton to grow up a little. At 18, Dalton had bragged insufferably that he could ride anything with four legs. Ben was on a regular visit to The Homestead. He waited until Dalton had a couple of friends with him, one his latest fawning ladylove, and had taken him up on his brag. He dared him to ride his new mare. Dalton didn't last 30 seconds on the horse. Ben added insult to injury by riding the horse away himself.

What Dalton hadn't known was that the mare Ben had been training was truly stubborn. She hated being held back. Ben knew that Dalton always rode with a tight rein. He had egged him on that day telling him how jumpy the horse was, so Dalton had held her in even more closely than normal. She went crazy and he ended up on the ground. Then Ben had talked to her gently for a minute, slid onto her with the reins totally loose, as she liked them. She walked away with hardly a hump. Henry and Hal got a big laugh out of the whole affair, feeling Dalton needed to come down a bit. Dalton had never really forgiven Ben, but they did have a kind of truce. Still Ben savored that face off enough that he loved seeing the look on Dalton's face each time he saw Ben on Peanut. Ben had kept her at first just to keep ribbing him, but he'd fallen under her spell. At 26 she was old enough now to go out to pasture, but he had grown to cherish her still cantankerous ways.

His thoughts were jerked back as Ann switched the topic to her plan to stay out West and look for work in Seattle. Just like Angie, he thought, drawn by the lights. Ben spun quickly toward her. "Back to the city? You miss it?"

"No," she told them, "I don't miss the city at all, but I need to earn a living. Seattle, I believe, holds the most opportunity for me. I'm staying out West specifically to be close to Em."

Then Dalton was off, explaining more about his move home and what it meant to him. He was a smooth storyteller and he kept his narrative interesting and light. Ben was left standing off to the side again. He wandered around studying Ann's charcoals. Dalton kept up his commentary until Hal and Em rejoined them. As they stepped out on the porch to say good-bye, Dalton pulled Ann off to the side and asked if he could come back and take her out to lunch the next Saturday. Ann readily agreed. She had enjoyed the evening and it would be great to get to know him better.

After Hal and Dalton had left, Ben seemed to be in a black mood. Em didn't notice, just excused herself and floated to her room. "Isn't it wonderful to see how happy love can make you at their age?" Ann asked.

"I hadn't planned to wait that long."

"Well, you may have to. You're not easy to talk to."

"I'm not a charmer like Dalton. I say what's on my mind."

"Well, there must not have been much on your mind tonight. I had to drag every word out of you."

"You were on my mind. You're responsible for getting Em to let loose of the past. She's never really been herself since Henry died." He reached out and his fingers trailed gently along her cheek. He was thinking how beautiful she looked. He had heard Dalton's invitation and her eager acceptance. He was kicking himself a bit for not making the first move. It was too late now to say anything. Ann had made her interest in Dalton too obvious.

He paused. Ann watched him, thinking he had something else to say but he just finished with "goodnight" and left.

As she went to her loft, Ann's walking was stiffer. Surely it was just because she was tired from the excitement of day. She wouldn't dwell on that. She had a date to think about. But somehow it was the touch of Ben's hand on her cheek that stayed with her as she fell asleep.

Dalton drove from Seattle and picked up Ann for lunch in town on Saturday. They enjoyed their time together and made plans for her to return the visit.

Ann drove to Seattle the following week and Dalton planned to spend his days primarily giving her a tour of the city. She didn't want any misunderstandings and made hotel reservations, despite Dalton's offer of the extra room at his apartment. She might be a little old fashioned but she liked to start things off slowly. The first day she watched him argue a case in court. He was confident and well prepared; his voice was clear and forceful. His arguments were presented with straightforward logic. Ann was impressed by his skill.

The judge must have been too, he ruled in Dalton's favor. He was in his element in the courtroom. Since he needed to escort his client, Ann had made it to and from courthouse herself. She was already seated when he arrived. That worked well because she had to admit to herself the M. S. was affecting her walking and she hadn't talked to him about that yet. She could still get around all right, but had to be conscious with each step to lift up her toes. If she was distracted and the toe dropped, she stumbled. Judging curbs was a constant challenge. Her leg had a mild tingling sensation like it was waking up.

After the day in court, the time was theirs. In Dalton's car they toured much of the city. Starting at Pioneer Square, he gave her a running history lesson on the city. The original city got so muddy he told her, they just buried it and moved up a floor. He promised her a tour of the Underground Seattle on her next trip. When they walked through the famous Farmer's Market, Ann took his arm. He certainly didn't seem to mind and that gave her the steadying influence she needed to walk more easily. Then they drove down the waterfront and watched the huge cranes unloading the ships. Dalton was able to make it all interesting with great stories to accompany each site.

Another day, they spent time relaxing and feeding the ducks on Lake Washington, and then they strolled arm and arm through the Japanese Gardens in the University of Washington Arboretum. They tried out several restaurants, one Ann particularly liked overlooked the canal leading to the locks. They watched boats going and coming from the salt water of the Puget Sound to the fresh water of Lake Washington. He told her they would come back again to see the salmon migrate up that route in the fall. Ann was enthralled with the water everywhere. Chicago had water too, but this seemed so much more picturesque, or maybe she admitted to herself, it was partly that she was taking some time away from her career to experience it. The mountains, though, were something Chicago didn't have and they made impressive backdrops wherever you looked.

Ann was having a great time. Dalton seemed to be, too. He was fun to be with, so attentive and thoughtful. It was almost over-whelming. He seemed content to let their relationship develop in its own time. Still, he made it clear he planned for it to continue with regular references to places he would take her another time. He made helpful suggestions, too, about potential employers.

The only negative note was his implication that she'd only need a temporary job, until she married. He'd backed off quickly when she took issue with his remark. But it did make her a little uneasy about his attitude.

They agreed to meet again the following weekend. Dalton explained that he liked to ride often and he had a horse boarded nearby. He would bring it with him to Morton.

Saturday Dalton arrived early pulling his trailer. The horse he unloaded was a big sorrel. It was long legged and slender. "A pure bred," he assured her, "and gentle enough for a child." They went to the pasture, Comanche came when she called. Dalton put the saddle on his back and cinched it up. He looked at the bridle Ann brought over with obvious disdain. He returned to the trailer and brought out one made of soft braided leather strips with sparkling silver trim. It was beautiful workmanship. She noticed for the first time really that the one Ben had given her and instructed her to use was big and bulky. The silver was scratched and worn. It was obviously built for pure practicality, not show. As Dalton slipped the bridle on Comanche, she protested weakly that Ben had been very specific that she only use this one bridle. Dalton laughed off her objection. As Ann mounted up, she noted that the back cinch was not yet hooked. He said it would be all right; they would stay to the flats. He tucked it up behind her saddle. Ann noted he did the same with his.

Dalton led the way out of the pasture. They tried several trails, then Dalton told her he knew of an area that he was sure Ben hadn't shown her. He took her higher into the hills along a well-used path to a gate she had seen, but not been through. A short way up the trail

Dalton turned, pushing through a cluster of underbrush. They quickly entered another world.

The ground was covered with needles so thick they dampened every sound. The horses plodding steps just seemed to fade away. The trees were immense. Most were at least ten feet in diameter; some looked nearly twice that size. They seemed to stretch up forever and all light coming in was filtered through their branches. It gave the scene a soft but slightly unearthly feeling. As they rode, Dalton explained that this was old-growth forest. All the rest of The Homestead had been logged once, 80–100 years ago, so although the trees were large, they didn't compare to these which had been here since before Columbus.

Ann was fascinated by the difference in the vegetation. There were trees that had fallen, nursery trees; Dalton called them. Young seedlings were growing all along them, but the dead trunks rotted away and left the roots exposed forming little teepees that held them suspended.

Often along the fallen trees grew large brown-topped fungus with lovely creamy undersides. They were shaped in fluted semi-circles and sprouted like stair-steps up the sides of the downed giants. Mushrooms were everywhere and came in every size. She found them from fingernail size to black and yellow dinner plates, in this climate where no direct sunlight would ever shine. Ann just wandered slowly from one wonder to another with Dalton walking along behind leading the horses and explaining her finds. Occasionally the cry of a startled bird could be heard to break the stillness. It was the most comforting, yet almost foreboding place she could imagine.

The day went quickly but it was another special experience that drew them closer. Before he helped Ann back into her saddle, Dalton took the opportunity of their closeness to kiss her. It wasn't the quick, but sweet, goodnight they had had in Seattle. It was long and passionate. To Ann the embrace was not unwelcome and the protecting cover of the darkened forest seemed to press them even more intimately together. As they rode home, Dalton suggested that she not mention to Ben where they had been. "He kind of considers this his own personal territory," he said. Ann realized that must be true or Ben would have taken her here on one of their rides.

Comanche had been a little less responsive to Ann today. She wondered if it was because the unfamiliar horse distracted him. Once they got back to the trails and headed home, he seemed to settle down. When they reached the far end of the pasture, Ann asked if Dalton wanted to race home. He was game. Comanche's short bunched muscles pushed him out front at the fir t jump, but the long legged racing stock of Dalton's Reggie took them past in a few bounds. Dalton stayed ahead for a while to show her he could, then pulled up a little to let Ann come along side. She tried to slow Comanche but he ignored her, redoubled his effort and ran past Reggie with everything he had. She pulled harder on the reins, but to no avail.

Ann was frightened. Comanche kept up the headlong pace to the edge of the corral, then he skidded to a jarring stop. The saddle flipped forward. Ann flew over her horse's neck and landed roughly on the ground with a yell of pain. Ben ran out of the barn as Dalton rode up and jumped from Reggie to her aid. They both demanded to know if she was all right, as they glared at each other over her prone form. She took quick stock. She hurt, she assured them, but didn't find anything broken.

Dalton turned angrily to Ben, "I knew you would give her too much horse!"

Totally ignoring Dalton, Ben faced Ann. He brought his hand forward and she noticed, he was holding the bridle she had been instructed to use. "Remember when I showed you how to saddle? The back cinch is intimidating to <u>some</u> people because you need to reach in close to the back feet and maybe the privates but it holds the saddle down for fast stops. Maybe you noticed." He added sarcastically. "The loose saddle is what through you off." Ann glanced at

Dalton and caught his sheepish look. Ben paid no attention and continued focusing on her. "Perhaps I should have explained in more detail about this bridle and Comanche. Comanche has good Arabian blood but I purchased him from a riding academy. He was so gentle, they used him as a kids' horse. Beginners are often frightened. If they're not watched they yank on the bit. Comanche had a sensitive mouth but their constant pulling toughened it. He learned to take a bit in his teeth and run for the barn when he got tired of the harassment. He is a fine horse but he was going to be destroyed, so I brought him here instead. This bit is special, you see how the mouthpiece has a big bump in it? That puts extra pressure on his pallet when you pull on the reins. With that, he minds without question. The sidepieces are extra long and sturdy. The reason I told you not to let anyone else ride him is because with those long sides and this bend in the mouthpiece a strong man could break his pallet. But that fancy do-dad you put on him gave you no control. He just chomped down on it and did as he pleased. If it doesn't suit you to use the equipment he needs, you can have a different horse." He turned and walked away.

Ben was angry with himself again. He should have told her about Comanche before so she would make intelligent decisions about her riding; instead of assuming she would always be riding with him around. That was jumping to conclusions. He could see now that the woman he was intrigued with because she seemed ready to leave the elegant clothes and city fancies behind was still easily caught up in Dalton's charm. He was a good-looking, fast-talking man, but city to the core and she obviously loved it. Ben wondered why he was kidding himself, taking more than a passing interest in her. On the other hand, he had fought and beaten Dalton on more than one occasion. He could do it again. He just needed to decide if Ann was worth the effort. More than that. Was it fair to her to take Dalton on, instead of letting her go after what she evidently liked? He had had his chance and let it go by.

Dalton helped Ann unsaddle. She removed the fancy bridle he had loaned her and returned it without comment. They didn't refer again to what happened, each just holding their thoughts as they got Reggie ready to transport. They did agree that they would like to see each other again. Dalton cautiously suggested that he could leave Reggie locally and come back next weekend to ride. He knew of a place he thought she would enjoy, off of The Homestead. Ann agreed to his suggestion with a smile.

The following Saturday, when Dalton arrived he found Ann ready. She made it clear without a word that Comanche was still her mount of choice. He was saddled and waiting with the back cinch fastened and the homely bridle adorning his muzzle. Dalton made no comment on her horse as he got Reggie ready. They rode down the driveway and then along the county road for some distance, ending up on another section of National Forest land. The Forest Service had cut firebreaks that the local horse folks used as bridle paths and they often had group rides or distance races, Dalton told her. Along the way they met a couple that knew Dalton, but most of the time they were by themselves. They kept up a pleasant conversation as they rode through the green landscape for several hours.

They followed along a steep bluff for some distance, then Dalton got down, tied his reins firmly to a sturdy branch and helped Ann down. "We'll leave the horses here," he said. Ann took off her saddle rope, removed Comanche's bridle and tied him as she'd been taught, so he could graze. Dalton had been busy removing his saddlebags, which looked heavily loaded. When he noticed what she had done, he looked a little taken aback. She saw that he didn't even have a rope. "Reggie is trained to stand," he said. Ann was cautiously trying out her legs. The stiffness from being in the saddle compounded her awkwardness. "You look like you're a little stiff from the ride. You better walk that out before we start."

Then her attention centered on a fairly steep, narrow trail cutting up toward the bluff top. Ann was pretty sure she could climb it if it didn't get any narrower. A walking stick for support would help. She looked around and found a branch that looked like it would do the job. But she resolved that the day had come to tell Dalton.

"How far?" she asked.

"Less than a quarter mile to the top."

"Then I'll work it out as we go," she said, thinking that a health discussion could wait that long and not upset his plans. "You lead."

Ann made frequent use of her branch. Dalton hadn't mentioned that the trail was steep and rough. By the time they reached the top she was desperate for a chance to sit. The view of Mt. Rainier was nice, but she felt it was not as special as the one from her favored cedar stump at the old cabin. Besides she was almost too exhausted to enjoy it. Dalton seemed uncomfortable, ignoring the view; he started unpacking his saddlebags. He pulled out stuffed game hens, bread, cheese, two long stemmed plastic glasses and a bottle of wine.

"I didn't realize you would get that tired. I thought you said you jogged and golfed in Chicago."

"I did. Things have changed for me though. I should have told you before, but I just didn't find the right moment. One of the reasons I left Chicago was a medical issue."

"A little convalescence, eh? Well, you should have just admitted you weren't quite back to top form yet. This could have waited."

"It's not a case of waiting. I was diagnosed with multiple sclerosis" She hurried on wanting to temper the bad news if she could. "It is the 'relapsing remitting' kind. That means I have these episodes that come on unexpectedly and fade away in most cases in a month or two. But I have no way of knowing if they will fade so I don't want to wait for anything. I want to experience everything I can now."

He seemed speechless. She probably hadn't handled this well. Somehow she couldn't seem to do this right, but then she hadn't had much practice, yet. To give him some time, she started laying out the lunch. "Are you familiar with M.S. at all? Is there anything you'd like to know? I don't mind talking about it."

"I can't think of anything," he said, reaching for the bottle of wine. He poured two glasses.

She accepted hers, but decided that she was really unsteady enough without much of that. She tried to move the conversation, commenting on the lovely view, but she couldn't get much out of him except one or two word answers. Is that how I affect Western men? She wondered. She had a sinking feeling that her blooming relationship with Dalton had suddenly wilted.

They managed to finish most of the lunch, Dalton drinking the wine by himself. As soon as the bottle was gone, he suggested they go down. He stuffed the leftovers back into his saddlebags and took off down the trail. He looked like he could use a walking stick. She found that she was still tired and fell quite a ways behind. She kept her eyes on the trail to be sure she wouldn't trip over any rough spots.

When she arrived at the bottom of the trail, she glanced up and realized from the devastated look on his face that he had been watching her struggle. He turned beet red at her glance. At least, she thought, he hadn't totally deserted her. He did have his saddlebags back in place, Comanche's bridle and saddle on, and her rope coiled. He avoided looking her in the eyes, just helped her onto Comanche. They had a silent trip home and there was no talk of another date.

CHAPTER 6

Over breakfast that Sunday morning, Em beamed as she told Ann that she and Hal would be going out of town Wednesday and be gone at least a week. They would be traveling to see some friends. Hal had a surprise stop scheduled, too, but Em hadn't been able to get him to hint at what that was about.

Em was obviously thrilled with the prospect of the trip. Ann decided that this break in routine was good for them both. It could be a catalyst to keep her promise to herself to get started on a serious job search. Since her plans with Dalton had fallen through she just hadn't been excited about heading back to Seattle. If she left the same day, she would have several weekdays to talk to businesses, then a few days rest and she could continue on the next week. "I'll go away too, to Seattle, if the place will be all right."

"Sure, it will be fine. Ben can handle everything. We won't worry about each other's schedule. Return will be flexible. After a week or so we can try cell phones just to check in."

They turned their conversation to more everyday things. Ann remembered then to ask how much logging was planned. Em's reply startled her, "Oh, we'll have to do a little logging sometime, but I hope we won't need to any time soon. I hate to see the timber come down. Even though Henry was a logger, I never got used to it. The look of a barren hillside that was lush a few days before is just sad.

This place was already logged when Henry and I married. We agreed that Henry would always work somewhere else, on someone else's land. That way, our place would grow back to some semblance of what it was before Henry's dad cut the original timber. It was all harvested about the turn of the century, except one small stand of old growth. Over the years some has been kept for pasture, but I love how much is forested. We have timber stands that are 80 to 90 years old. Some land I planted, taking tiny trees from Henry's logging shows and bringing them here. Henry thought it was a little eccentric of me but now those trees are over 50 years old and coming along nicely."

Ann had trouble following the story. She had been so surprised by Em's first remark; she couldn't get past it. She let Em wander off without replying. Em didn't seem to know there was timber coming off her land right now! What's more she would obviously object to cutting her trees, if asked.

After some thought, Ann headed down to the barn for a frank talk with Ben. His back was toward her as she entered the barn. He was graining the horses. "Hey, that's my job," she called out. The man quickly turned, obviously startled; it wasn't Ben. He was a stranger.

"Well now, little lady. I wouldn't want to take your work, but I didn't know there was another hand on board, especially such a pretty one. I just took a few weeks off. I didn't know I'd be replaced. Most folks call me Bronco. It's how I met Ben, bronc riding I mean. He's some rider ain't he? I mean the way he just talks them horses down is something to see."

"He was with the rodeo?"

"He started riding the circuit after he dropped out of college. He would've been good at that engineering stuff; too bad he quit. Anyway, he was hardly more than a kid and I sorta adopted him. Now I live down the road a piece and he sees to it I get a little work for spendin' money. It gives him extra time when he's got somethin' else goin'. But, if you want to work too dearie, I'll share."

Ann shook her head, still flabbergasted at finding the old fellow there. She paused to assimilate the barrage of information coming her way. "Where is Ben?" She finally asked.

"Didn't say. Hardly ever does."

"But his truck's here."

"Yah, but Peanut isn't. Haven't you ever noticed, lots of times he just goes off on her?"

Well, she thought, she often saw the truck there late and early but she just assumed he kept long hours. It never occurred to her he could be out overnight with the horse. Her thoughts were interrupted.

"You must be that little Ann gal he's talked about. Didn't know you was such a pert little thing."

She didn't want to hear what Ben had said about her, with all the silly things she had pulled in the last few months. She thanked Bronco and headed back to the house. Em said she knew Ben was gone. She went on without a breath to another story. She was certainly in a talkative mood today.

"Ben takes off sometimes for a day or two, always has. At times he just goes down to the old cabin. He maintains his great-grand-mother's grave. A while back he had a new headstone made, too. The original wooden one was worn beyond recognition."

"I thought this was our family's place. I've been meaning to ask you, who was Martha Longley? Wasn't Mary great-grandmother's name? Are you saying Ben is related to me?"

"Whoa! You're as fast a talker as I am. Let me answer this pile of questions before you stack on any more. Martha was your great-grandfather John's first wife. She died shortly after the birth of their daughter, soon after they settled here. John later married Mary. John and Martha's daughter, Laura, was raised here but married and moved away. Your grandfather Henry stayed on the land and inherited The Homestead. He had two children, your mother and Henry

Jr. Your Mom also moved away but Henry stayed on here and kept the land.

So, Ben is a relative, kind of shirttail. Let's see. To you, I guess he'd be about a half-second cousin. We could figure it out for sure, if it matters."

"It doesn't really. So how did Ben end up here?"

"Henry and I stayed in close touch with Laura's daughter, Elizabeth. She was a rebellious girl. Never married when she found out she was pregnant. That was pretty scandalous in those days, but she never hesitated. She just settled down and tried to b : a good mother. We liked Liz. She and her son, Ben, came here a lot. From the time he was little he loved this place. When he got older he spent summers with us and any other chance he got. Then his Mom & Grandparents were killed in an accident and he stayed with us for a while."

Em started to move off, saying, "I don't know what got into me. I'd better hush though, on the subject of Ben. He is very insistent on his privacy. Anything else you'd like to know, you'd best ask him."

Ann decided to be patient on the logging issue until she could talk to Ben. Meanwhile, she headed back out to see if Bronco could use any help. He said, "Sure." Probably, she thought, to have a fresh ear to hear his stories, but I don't mind that. Bronco announced that they should clean the chicken house. This was the first chore that really got her hands, and everywhere else, dirty. She suspected that this was some kind of a test on Bronco's part. That was O.K. Little obstacles had been thrown in her way for as long as she could remember. She had gotten over them. She was certain she could master a little chicken guano.

A few minutes later she was tempted to revise that thought. While she avoided foul language, she'd heard the phrase "that's chicken shit" often enough and now she knew why it was so derisive. It was not just the smell, which was bad enough although a lot of the stuff had dried, reducing the odor; but the flat shovel she was using to scrape it up raised a putrid dust. She tried to hold her breath but even after stepping out to breathe it settled in her throat. The taste was enough to make you gag. Bronco noticed her problem with a little smirk and gave her a bandanna to tie over her mouth and nose. That made all the difference. She caught a glimpse of his smirk and it firmed her resolve. He seemed surprised at the lengths she went to with no complaining. She doubted the place had ever been that clean. She intended to be taken seriously, as real help.

They worked on a few other things. Bronco chuckled as she tried to learn the new skills she needed for the chores. In the end, however, she could operate a barbed wire stretcher and get a full pitchfork of hay. He would just give her a pointer or two as they worked. He was very patient, demonstrating and explaining. She was easily exhausted these days, but he joined her without comment whenever she felt the need for a short rest.

No matter what they were doing the stories poured out in a relentless flood. He told about rodeo life, places he'd been, great riders, and great animals he had known. They all held Ann enthralled but those about Em and Ben were the most fun to hear. He showed no reserve in telling stories involving either of the pair. He started many stories, "Did I ever tell you," as if Ann had known him more than a few hours.

"Fiero," he declared, "was the greatest rodeo bull ya' ever seen." He went on to tell how the bull had never been beaten. He had thrown Ben repeatedly, but Ben always went back for more. When Ben left the rodeo circuit, he bought the bull and they retired together.

"What use is an old bull? Why would he buy him?"

"Well, ya'd have to ask Ben for sure. I figure Fiero was getting older and one day soon some one was gonna ride him. Ben just didn't want that to happen. He let ol' Fiero retire at the top."

"That sounds pretty sentimental, for a guy like Ben."

Bronco gave her a disgusted look. The wad of tobacco moved from one cheek to another in a jump. He let spew a long disgusting stream. Finally he just shook his head and started to walk away. "Ya sure do have a lot to learn 'bout men," he tossed over his shoulder.

Ann started to protest his judgment, but thought about Martha's gravestone and the wild flowers. Maybe Ben was a little tenderer than he cared to let on.

Bronco had told her they'd finished everything he wanted to get done. He would take off tomorrow if she'd feed the stock. She had agreed she would if Ben hadn't returned.

Ann's arm snaked up searching for the alarm. She couldn't find it and the shrill calls continued. She came slowly to her senses. She hadn't had this much trouble waking since she arrived her away from the Chicago rush. The little bird kept whistling. Em had told her the name, but there were just too many and she couldn't remember them all. No matter, its insistent call was a great replacement for a buzzing clock.

She hopped up and looked out the window. It would probably be another cool day but at least it wasn't raining, not yet anyway. Her usual good humor was slightly dampened by the prospect of talking to Ben but she started out resolutely. She found a note from Em that she had run to town and wouldn't be back until afternoon so that left Anne's day free for working things out with him.

Two hours later she admitted he probably wasn't coming back today. It was a good chance to look at the logging operation and see what she could learn. She hadn't paid that much attention the first time she'd seen the site. She packed a lunch and some 'bird watching' binoculars in her saddlebags, thinking she would make a day of it.

Without really knowing why, Ann approached the logging area slowly. She picketed Comanche. As she approached on foot, she could hear machinery running. From the shelter of the woods she looked out onto the cleared area and saw that more trees had been cut since the last time she was here. There was a logging truck with a built-on crane sitting in the center of the area. She saw movement near another machine and went back for her saddlebags and binoculars.

There was no one in the truck. The movement she had seen was Ben. He was operating a machine that had a spool of cable on the back, a blade on the front and huge rubber tires. The machine could turn in very tight spaces, revolving almost 90 degrees to change directions. It was very narrow in the middle like the two parts of an ant's body and connected, sort of like a hinge, only there were some kind of hydraulic cylinders tied in. The monstrous tires appeared to be about 5 feet high and allowed it to climb over stacks of branches, small stumps and pretty good-sized logs. The most amazing thing was the way the front half of the 'body' would tilt to go over an obstacle, while the back was flat on the ground. So it would be bending side-to-side and left to right at the same time at seemingly impossible angles.

Ben used the machine to pull in the downed trees to stacks near the loader. After hauling in a log Ben would drive the machine near another downed tree. Then he would jump off and grab the metal cable on the spool and pull it out. It was stiff and must weigh a lot. The tendons in his arms bulged as he worked. His muscles weren't the massive overstated bulk of a weight lifter. They were working fibers, sinuous, stretched taut and straining with his exertions. His shirt was soaked with sweat down his backbone and across his shoulders. The way it stuck to him only emphasized his strength.

When he reached the log he wanted, he worked the end of the line around and somehow fastened it. Then he fought his way through the discarded branches back to the pulling machine. Ben started the reel turning. The cable tensed sometimes catching on branches, breaking them and tossing them out of the way like toothpicks. Popping and cracking filled the air. As the log was yanked toward the machine it jumped over little stumps and broken limbs. Bark ripped from the heaving carcass, but it still snaked toward the relentless machine. When he had it close enough to slightly lift the leading end, Ben gunned the puller off across the clearing to one of his stacks.

Ann could see why Em avoided logging. Not only was the clearing a tangle of ripped and shredded limbs; but even more tormenting was the noise. It was deafening. The trees screamed in protest against being towed. They fought every inch of the way. It was no wonder loggers were always portrayed as such tough men. She was stunned at the stamina it took for Ben to get the trees out by himself. It was incredible. It would be an amazing demonstration of individual achievement—if it weren't theft!

Ben was sorting the logs into piles as he brought them in. She finally deduced it was based on size and type. Some of the trees had alder bark and went to a separate pile. She watched fascinated for well over an hour as he hauled the biggest timber to a stack near where the log truck was parked.

Then he turned off the pulling machine. He climbed into the truck cab and fired it up. Soon he was using the truck's crane to load the trailer. The process captured her totally and Ann stayed in her hiding place, slowly eating her lunch. He had to grab each log just right, not necessarily at the middle, but at its center of balance. The big end was a lot heavier, she noted. Sometimes he had to adjust the hold or it would get overbalanced and drag on the ground. When he finally got one up it might swing precariously, unwilling to join the growing stack on the truck destined for saws at a mill, she guessed. Other times he would gasp two smaller logs at a time. They appeared to want to go in different directions but the pinchers of crane would close and slowly bring them into harmony to rest on the growing load on the truck. The process was tricky and it took him quite a while to get a full load. Then he folded up the big arm that grabbed the logs and drove the truck out. As she watched, he opened a gate at the back of the clearing. He drove through and re-closed it. She knew from their rides that he was going onto a National Forest logging road. He drove away.

The logging was going slowly. Ben was familiar with all phases of the process from his summers working with Henry. Still there were parts of the job that Henry had discouraged him from doing. Ben was never sure if it was because of safety or the extra wear it would cause on the equipment that Henry was avoiding. At any rate he was learning some things as he went. He had been careful with the falling; only dropping trees on days with no wind. Then he had started working one area at a time, limbing and pulling the timber to a landing for loading. He didn't have much experience with the self-loader, since that was one job Henry insisted on doing himself. Still, he could get the job done with patience. The difference in profit was huge, so he stuck it out. He had the time he needed to get it done.

Although he knew he should keep his mind strictly on his work, his thoughts drifted. Ann and Dalton were finished, he knew, since Dalton had been by last Saturday night to pour out his troubles. So he had another chance with her in theory but she had never even glanced in his direction. That was largely his own fault, as he had encouraged her to think of him as nothing more than a horse wrangler. Now he had to live with that. If he could just get her to come to his hide-away, she might think again. He would need some way to get her there; it couldn't just be "want to come home for dinner?" She would undoubtedly say no. Why would someone of her background be interested? Especially now, since their relations had been a little strained after the scene with Dalton over Comanche. He knew his jealousy had partly fired that row, but couldn't mend it now. With no solution in mind he finished up the load and drove the truck out to the mill.

Ann packed up and rode home without making sense of what Ben was doing. Why was he keeping this from Em, if not to cheat her? She didn't want to think badly of Ben but was at a loss for another explanation. She had heard plenty about senior citizen rip-offs and knew it was far from uncommon. When Ann got home she once again brought up logging with her aunt. Ann didn't tell her what she had seen, just asked about the logging process. Em knew all the answers she sought. Anne learned that the Forestry Service let out rights to use their logging roads. The logging permit process was controlled by the Department of Natural Resources.

Ann expressed curiosity about the land itself. Em gladly showed her a map that had M Bar M land outlined in red. It clearly showed that the land being logged was a part of The Homestead. That raised a question she had meant to ask for a while. "Why is this the M Bar M? You always call it The Homestead."

"Henry, Sr. changed the name to M Bar M in memory of the two wives he outlived. So that's the official name. But the family never got used to that so they always called it The Homestead amongst themselves and it just stuck."

"Are the Forestry roads numbered instead of named?" Ann pointed to the road she believed Ben was using. It said #8870.

"Yes. They have roads everywhere through their land to give fire-breaks and logging access. There are so many only a number system is practical."

There were figures hand-written in on several spots on the home-stead land. Ann thought she had identified the section Ben was logging. That one showed 500,000. Ann asked what that meant.

Em explained that she and Ben decided to have the timber cruised. "That means that the amount of standing timber is esti-mated. Right now, for example, big timber of export grade is selling for about $1000 for each thousand board feet. Smaller timber is less, of course, and it's good to support local business. You remember" she said, "the two mills I showed you in Morton that make 2 by 4's? Well, you can sell to them but it pays less than exporting. The exporters only take large trees. It's sad but because of the financial difference, the best U. S. timber goes overseas. Of course, most peo-ple don't clear the $1000 anyway, there's a lot of expense. The logging expenses usually run about half. If we ever have to log any Homestead land, we'll have an advantage because Ben learned working with Henry. We kept the equipment and he can use all of it. He's an O.K. faller, too, although I think he takes more risks than he should."

Ann was staggered by the math. She wasn't sure of the size of the clearing, having no way to judge acres. But with Ben doing all the work himself, if a most of the logs were sold for export, he could make almost half a million dollars on one 10 acre section! For a ranch hand, well for most everyone, that is a lot of money. Em's money.

Ann felt betrayed. She had been duped, leaving her city bred cynicism behind. Ben was not at all what he appeared, in more ways than one. He had some big ideas, he was just careful not to let on. He had to know Em would never turn him in. It was up to Ann to protect her aunt, although she was sickened by the idea.

Ann slept restlessly but by morning her mind was made up. She didn't say a word to Em. She called the Forest Service, without giving her name. She simply told them that she believed that someone was illegally cutting timber and using road #8870 to take it out.

Ann rode out again and watched all day as Ben trimmed limbs and then pulled in logs. He worked hard and she could see that this was a slow process for one man. It explained his recent disappearances. Late in the day a pick-up stopped by the gate. It was the pale green Ann recognized as a Forestry truck. A man honked until he had Ben's attention and walked over to talk to Ben for quite a while. Then they both started to laugh. He clapped Ben on the back, went back to his rig and drove away. Ann couldn't believe it. Ben must have his story down pat. She would have to face up to a talk with Em to make this stop.

That night she told Em what Ben was doing.

"Why that scamp. He knows how I hate to face logging, so he's just doing it on the sly."

"Why wouldn't he tell you? Em, I know you care about him, but he's robbing you. I have to admit I called the Forest Service today and asked them to check out what's going on. I felt you wouldn't do anything to hurt Ben, so I thought I'd just have it investigated without saying anything. It didn't work out, though. Ben must have a good story because the man left with a lot of joking and back slapping."

Em collapsed into a chair. After a moment she gathered herself and started in on Ann. "My dear, you owe Ben an apology. He is so insistent about his privacy that he shares some blame, but you cannot make decisions for me. I'm getting old, I know, but I'm not gone yet. Ben has rights on this place. When Henry was sick at the end, we had no health insurance. I went through our savings pretty fast, and then I mortgaged the land. After...when I was alone, I was having a hard time. I thought I might default and lose this place, but Ben bailed me out. I started by just selling him the old cabin site but as time went on we decided a partnership was better. I do all the paperwork; deal with the state, the Feds, or whoever. I keep the books, too. Ben runs the place. Usually he has me get any permits we need but this logging must be unusual. He has a reason and I don't care what it is. He is one of the best men you will ever meet! You will apologize!" Then she jumped swiftly up, clearly distraught, and went to her room.

CHAPTER 7

Ann felt sick. She had upset Em terribly. She knew she was often headstrong but this time she was convinced that Em had misinterpreted the situation. If her aunt normally got the permits, why was this time different? What kind of a surprise called for this much money? Why would he just disappear and not tell Em what he was doing? It just felt wrong. Even partners could be cheated. She was angry, too, that Ben had acted "the ranch hand" part; never letting on that he was a part owner. Still Em was right that she needed to confront Ben. She resolved to face him first thing in the morning. Once this issue was settled, she would leave for Seattle. Maybe it would be good to get away for a while and let things simmer down with Em.

Ann came slowly awake. The sound was drifting in on her dreamily. Plip. Plop. Plop…Her eyes flew open as it hit her. Rain! She couldn't believe it. Doesn't this country ever have a dry season? She got up grumpily and started picking out clothes for the day. She looked out the loft window and noticed Ben's pick-up by the barn. At least she would be able to take care of that today.

A few minutes later, she had to revise her idea. Just as she stepped out on the porch shrouded in her rain clothes and ready to face him, Ben rode off on Peanut. She returned to the house, secretly thankful for the reprieve, and started packing for her trip.

She called Bill Caldwell and told him she wouldn't be able to come in this week to work on his ads. He assured her that wasn't a problem. The work she had done was already paying off for him. "A couple of the sketches you drew as proposals for potential advertisers really went over well. One of the buyers even signed a two-year contract. That may not sound like much but with your other work, I've increased my advertising income by almost 10%. That means a lot to me. I'm glad to hear from you, because I was going to call you on another issue. That little Western wear store in Chehalis wants permission to use your ad copy in the Olympian. That's a daily newspaper a lot people read around this area. What do you think?"

"Bill, I created that for you. I believe you have the right to say where it's used and how."

"Well, we didn't talk about it up front. I appreciate you taking that attitude. What I think would be fair is a small fee each time it's used. A little store like that is always cash poor. You and I could split whatever comes in."

"That sounds more than reasonable to me. You do what you think is right. I'm sure I'll be happy with it. I'll come in next week and see what else you need." Ann hung up feeling great about how things were going for Bill and for her, too. She had forgotten how good it felt to be appreciated by your employer. Besides, the work was fun.

Her packing finished, Ann moved out to the porch swing. It was a favorite spot for her. She always enjoyed the calming affect of just rocking there. Today it had the added benefit of letting her avoid talking to Em until she had seen Ben. Hours had passed but there was no sign of him and the rain kept drizzling.

Em finished her preparations and left to meet Hal with a hug goodbye and no further comment on the previous day's confrontation. Ann finally admitted to herself that she was procrastinating to avoid facing Ben. There were a couple of likely places she could look for him and she resolved to get started. It was already after four, however, when she saddled up and rode out, dressed again to shed the sky's soggy offerings. The logging show would be her first stop, she thought, then she would try the old cabin.

She entered the clearing openly this time. There was no log truck. The pulling machine was standing idle in the middle of the cut area. She was turning to leave when Comanche whinnied. His greeting was answered. It sounded like it came from the trees beyond. It was hard to tell. The slithering sounds of the rain gear each time she or the horse moved didn't help any. Her eyes carefully scanned the edges of the trees, but she saw no one. Then she heard a call accompanied by a barely visible hand waving near a log pile.

There was a lot of downed timber between her and Ben. She knew something was wrong, but couldn't imagine what. She tied Comanche and worked her way through the criss-cross of trees. Ben was lying on the ground, in just his jeans and a hickory shirt. This shirt had the sleeves cut off above the elbows, and he was thoroughly soaked.

"My foot's caught. Under a tarp just into the woods over there are two chain saws. Bring me the small one."

She fought her way to where he indicated over and around logs and clinging branches. Even the street curbs had seemed daunting at times but they were nothing compared to this. The branches went every which way. Step on one end with a foot and the other end popped up just in time to hook the other leg. Slam! You were thrown flat before you could blink. She made herself slow down and measure each step. Still, the effort left her exhausted. She hated being limited in what she could accomplish. At times like this, it wasn't just tingling. She ached and felt that with each step she had less control over her legs. By the time she found the tarp, she had to sit down and rest. She noticed that there was a plaid wool coat wrapped in the tarp and decided she had better take that as well. Even though it was a relatively warm day, there was a strong breeze. She was sweating now with the rain gear still on and the exertion, but she had been a little chilled while she was riding. Ben had looked really cold with a grayish tinge to his face.

The trip back was much worse with the saw and coat to handle. She fell a couple of times. When she finally made it, Ann collapsed beside him and handed him the coat. He started to shrug off the need but gave in when she pointed out that he was shivering. She helped him strip off the wet shirt and struggle into the coat.

Ben was trapped in an awkward position. It took them both to start the saw. First, Ben worked the choke and held it steady, while Ann tried to pull the starter rope. That was a bust. It gave her more appreciation for his strength. So they shifted, she braced the saw around to an angle where he could reach the rope. It fired on his second attempt. The scream was deafening.

He signaled Ann to stand back. The saw bit into the log throwing chips behind it at an amazing speed. He made a cut to each side of his foot and shoved the piece off to free himself. Then the nightmare of fighting the downed timber started again. They held on to each other, sort of taking turns providing support when one or the other would stumble. Once they went down in a jumble. Ben used his arm to catch Ann, instead of breaking his fall. He cracked his head on a protruding limb. Ann was frightened, but he assured her he was fine, just wanted to lay there for a minute. He pulled his arms more tightly around her. She laid her head on his chest, too worn out to argue.

A few minutes later he told her he was ready to go on. Ben had headed for the woods, since that was closest. Peanut was tied there, still saddled.

"Good thing she's patient," he said. "Been here all day." Ben climbed shakily into the saddle and pulled Ann up behind. As they rode over to Comanche, Ben tried to explain. "Wasn't planning to do any work today. Didn't wear corks."

She interrupted him, "Corks?"

"Boots—nails in the soles. To walk logs."

Ann saw that he was wearing his cowboy boots. "So you tried to walk a log?" He nodded. "Why were you out here anyway?"

"Wrenches on the Mountain Goat." He gestured, as he spoke, toward the machine Ann thought of as the pulling machine.

"Walked a log near the bottom of cold deck."

"That's the stack of logs I found you by?"

"Yah. I slipped. Deck shifted. No one knew where I was, figured they'd find my bones some day."

As Ann slid off Peanut she saw that Ben was starting to shake again. Once she was aboard Comanche though, Ben took off at a good pace. When they reached the fork in the trail he didn't head back to the house, but up toward the old growth. They quickly came to the gate that led to that section. Before Ben said a word she slipped off and moved toward the gate, but she paused. Ben was shivering again and she wondered about his judgment. "Why are we heading this way? Why not back to the house?"

"Peanut knows the way. Open the gate."

Ann did as he asked, but she didn't feel comfortable about the way he was acting. True, he never had much to say but somehow his terse sentences were different. She was worried.

They headed up a narrow trail along a rocky bluff. It was the same trail that she'd ridden with Dalton, but they didn't turn into the old-growth. After the first few yards, they were climbing steeply over a rough trail. The ground dropped off so sharply to their right she didn't think the horses could get down into the big timber if they tried. As they went Ben used one hand or the other to continually rub his legs. She noticed he clung to the saddle horn with the other, something she never thought she'd see. He had to be feeling the cold very deeply.

The climb seemed long, as tired as she was, but she supposed it wasn't really that far, just rough. When they came out on the top of the trail and through another gate, she was looking down at a remarkable view. A field spread out in all directions. The sides of the valley rose steeply to form a shape like a bowl. They had entered through a low pass. High, rocky bluffs enclosed the rest of the depression. This was a little world unto itself. There was only one other potential exit, for any one except a mountain goat or rock climber. That was near where a stream flowed in. It came over high bank with a pretty waterfall but it wasn't a towering cliff like the rest of the walls. Coming here seemed like a really bad idea, even if there was someone here, which there appeared to be.

To their right, resting on a gentle knoll, was a small cabin, a barn, another little out building and some corrals. Peanut headed eagerly down. Ann closed the gate and followed noticing it was immediately becoming darker and colder. Here the sun set earlier, and was already below the edge of the bluffs. The only sign of hope was lights. They were on in the cabin, so at least there was someone around.

Ben slid off his horse but was hardly able to stand. Ann jumped down and ran to help him, calling out to whoever lived here. "There's no one," he said. They staggered onto the porch, she started to knock but Ben just reached for the knob. He couldn't seem to get it so she twisted the knob and called out again. Ben was no sooner inside then he collapsed, started shivering even more violently and curled up in a ball. He wouldn't respond to her.

She called again louder, but decided even in his delirium he was right. No one was there. They were alone. She looked into the bed-room. There was a big comforter folded at the foot of the bed. She ran for it. She lay the covers over him; but feeling the chilled rug under her hand, thought better of it. Bunching part of the blanket against his back, spreading out the rest she kneeled on it. She grabbed his curled legs and with what felt like the end of her strength she heaved. Success! He rolled onto the padding. She pulled the quilt tightly around him, covering him entirely including his head.

Next she decided to start a fire in the big wood stove. She man-aged to get that going using the matches in a handy wall holder and plenty of the kindling stacked nearby. At least the place was well organized.

What else? Wet clothes are bad; no putting it off. She went back to the bedroom. At least the owner was a man. She silently apologized to him as she dug through the dresser and found a sweat suit, heavy socks and in the attached bathroom, a towel. Returning to the human cocoon, she pealed back the covers from Ben's legs. She rubbed vigorously to warm his stiffened limbs, trying to get him to stretch out so the pants would come off. It didn't work. Finally she went looking for scissors. She found a drawer with tools that included a pair of 'cut anything' snips and took them. She pulled on the boots, finally releasing the right. His injured foot must have swollen because he groaned when she tugged on that one. In desperation, she cut the boot along the seam, hoping it could be repaired. He'd just have to deal with her decision, she thought. She slit his pants, worked them off and dried his legs. With a struggle she got the loose sweats on. She re-covered Ben and collapsed on the sofa. There was no sign of a phone. It seemed unlikely this cabin in the middle of nowhere would have one.

Ann studied the place while she rested. Up until now she hadn't really had time. The rooms were simply furnished but comfortable. Besides the electric lights, there were several kerosene lamps. There was a large bookcase filled with several reference books and interesting mixture of authors: O'Henry, Pasternak, Dumas, Clavell. There was some lighter reading too like L'Amour's westerns. A First Aid manual caught her eye and she quickly looked up Hypothermia.

"Caused by prolonged exposure to cold or wearing damp clothing in cold conditions. Signs: pale, puffy face, listless, often drowsy. In severe cases breathing becomes slow and shallow, muscles stiff, the victim may be unconscious, heartbeat may slow or stop altogether."

"Don't die on me!" she silently screamed at him. She wanted him to stop hurting Em, not…She jerked her mind back to the book.

"Treatment: If suspected requires immediate medical attention."

Fat Chance! She thought.

"Give victim warm drinks, cover head from which as much as 20 percent of heat loss takes place."

"Well so far I've done O.K. on you," she told the unmoving bump.

"Young people are warmed in a bath. For the elderly, warm slowly in a room about 78 degrees with layers of heat reflecting material such as space blankets. In extreme conditions, body warmth can be used. Caregiver will remove clothing and enter sleeping bag with victim. Focus heat around the chest cavity."

Something about the word caregiver triggered her mind. The horses. She still had on her rain pants and slipped her jacket back on. The pair was grazing not far from the porch. She gathered their reins and led them to the barn. Stripping their saddles and bridles, she started to let them out into a side pen when a huge animal appeared. She could be wrong, but she judged from his size and bulk that this monster was a bull. She quickly decided she didn't want to know what lurked in any other pen. She decided to leave the horses in stalls until she could be sure they could be let out safely. She dried them off a little with some pieces of burlap. The minute she opened the grain bid the bull began bellowing. Maybe he wasn't as mean as he looked. She cautiously gave him a measure, too. He immediately quieted and came over to eat. She tried a timid scratch between his horns and was rewarded with a contented nuzzle on her hand as he munched his treat.

Suddenly one of a series of bins above his feed trough opened and a good measure of grain poured down. Ann realized with a start that it was an automatic feeding system. The bull, she thought, had a bit of a smirk on his face, he'd conned her into giving him a double measure night. She must be going nuts moving from talking to horses to thinking she was getting teased by a bull!

On the way back to the house she saw a back porch. She could hear a motor running near by, but didn't take time to check it out. She entered through the rear of the cabin, finding that door unlocked too. The little porch was hung with coats, other outdoor gear and a stocking hat. She removed her rain gear and took the cap.

In the main room she checked Ben and slipped the cap on his head. The shivering had given way to slow, shallow breathing. That didn't seem like a good sign. She built up the fire again, although the room was warming up nicely. As she sat down, all the lights went out. It was totally silent. The almost unnoticed sound of the motor had died. The stillness chilled her more than the cold ride. She sensed how really alone she was. She fleetingly thought of trying to light a lamp. Instead she decided to do what had been on her mind since reading the First Aid book. She removed her clothes down to her bra and panties and crawled under the covers. Ann unzipped Ben's coat and slipped inside. She put her arms as far around him as she could and tucked her face to his still chilled chest. She wasn't sure which one of them was being comforted. She was scared and felt the tears begin to flow. The last thing she remembered was feeling guilty. He wasn't supposed to be wet!

CHAPTER 8

Ann awoke languidly, feeling warm and safe. Strong arms held her gently. Slowly it dawned on her where she was and who held her. He was breathing normally now, but obviously still sleeping off yesterday's trauma. She was relieved. That gave her a chance to get out of this potentially compromising position. She slipped out of his embrace, grabbed her clothes and used the bathroom to freshen up and dress. The lights were working again and she thought she heard the generator running, at least that's what she assumed it was. That was odd since there was no sign that the missing owner had returned. Ben still hadn't stirred when she went back to the living room. She wasn't sure how long he needed to be kept warm but decided to relight the fire. There was a chill in the morning air. While getting the blaze started she tried to ignore the rumbles in her stomach. She was starved having missed dinner last night. The kitchen, however, was a mystery. There was a wood range, a hand pump and a water faucet at the sink, but no refrigerator. She decided her growling tummy could hold on a little longer. Maybe Ben would wake before she was hungry enough to paw through a stranger's cupboards.

Ann wanted to see what the place looked like in the daylight and slipped outside. She could tell the cabin wasn't very old, not like The Homestead. The construction was simple but the windows, siding and roofing were modern. There was some kind of small antenna protruding off the peak. The little home had a wide, open porch in the front and the enclosed one she had entered through the back last night.

The surrounding hills were even more impressive this morning. The rising sun glinted off the craggy turrets that flanked the valley. Scattered along the route of the stream there was an occasional scrub tree. The rest of the floor of the basin was covered with long unkempt grass, that at this point in the season was losing it's green. It looked like it was drying into hay. There were no stumps or signs of clearing. It appeared that this open area was natural. That surprised her. She had assumed this whole part of the state was evergreen forest and dense underbrush, since that was all she had seen.

Ann turned to the barn and could now see how the small fenced pastures worked. She went to the barn and got the horses. As she led Comanche and Peanut into the vacant pasture, the bull put in an apparently hopeful appearance, greeting them with his mournful bellow.

At first Ben believed he was having a realistic dream. He recognized the room, but he was on the floor and couldn't remember getting there. He hadn't had an experience like that since he stopped drinking over ten years ago. Little by little memories of yesterday returned, up to the point they had started up the trail to the cabin. After that things were blank. He was alone now, he hoped Ann hadn't tried getting back to the main house in the dark. He could see one cut boot and his jeans lying near him and he was wearing sweats, so he knew she had worked on warming him up. The First Aid Manual was on the couch. The fire was burning a fresh log, so she was still around somewhere. That brought a smile. It had been somewhat risky heading up here instead of to the house. It was a decision made when he was only partly coherent. On the other hand, it could be the best idea he'd had in a long time. It gave him the chance he wanted to let Ann see his place.

Ben got up but found it was painful to put weight on his swollen left foot and ankle. He hopped his way to the bedroom and took out one of the two adjustable length canes behind the door. He noted that the bed had not been slept in. The little couch wasn't long enough to stretch out on. Had she stayed up all night? With the use of the cane he got around the house pretty well. He slowly cleaned up. He decided that today he would wear something other than a hickory shirt. When he was dressed he worked his way to the kitchen and put on some coffee.

He was setting at the table sipping his first cup when Ann returned. "Coffee?" He asked as she stepped through the back door. She accepted with only a slight hesitation. He stayed at the table and told her where to find cups.

"How are you feeling?"

His answered with a little question in his voice. "Not bad, considering. The coffee helps. Probably be pretty much O.K., except for the ankle, once I get a little breakfast in me."

Ann sensed he was about to start asking some questions and got up quickly. "I'd better pick up the mess." She moved to the living room, put away the First Aid Manual and folded the quilt. She gathered up the boots and jeans and then paused. After a glance his direction, she junked them in the big wastebasket he indicated with a shrug.

When she came back to the table he voiced what was foremost on his mind. "What brought you out to the logging show yesterday? It sure was lucky for me, but unexpected."

Ann's heart skipped a beat. It seemed pretty odd to spend the night in a man's arms and then tell him you thought him a thief and guilty of conning an old woman. Oh, well. She had never been one to hide from an issue, except she chided herself, this M.S. issue with Ed.

She didn't want to think about that now. She looked Ben in the eye, wanting to see the reaction on his face.

"Why are you logging, without Em's knowledge or permission? I know you have some kind of partnership arrangement, but it's still not right."

"That got you curious, did it?" He started to laugh, then brought himself up short. "You didn't tell her did you?"

"Yes, I did!" His concern confirmed her suspicions. "I called the Forest Service, too. Does that worry you?"

"Worry, no, but it does upset me a little."

"Well, it didn't upset Em but her opinion at this point doesn't really mean anything. Most people who are being swindled are totally trusting of the thief."

His reaction was nothing like she expected. He wasn't trying to defend himself. He had first looked a little sad that she had told Em and now slightly amused that she had called the Forest Service. Well, she supposed the loss of that much money could be disappointing, and calling in the Feds had been a bust. She waited stiffly for him to say something.

He didn't seem ready to answer her, so she bored in with more questions. "If she normally takes care of paperwork why go around her for permits? Why didn't tell anyone where you were those days, unless you were trying to hide what you're doing?"

"Has Em ever shown you the inside of the big roll top desk in her room?"

"No! That has nothing to do with this. You can't just avoid answering me."

"Someday, have her show you the desk and I think you'll get a shock. Anyway, a while back I was in the desk…"

"What were you doing in her room? What right…?"

"Calm down a second and hear me out." He answered with an irritating chuckle. "I went into the desk to look at some of the joint records, which she keeps. She had a folder there with a collection of information on small, used motor homes. She was highlighting some that I assumed she was interested in looking at. I think she and Hal are planning to do a little traveling. I decided they shouldn't buy a used, high mileage unit. There's too much chance of a break down. Em is thinking of the expense. In many ways she still thinks about money like she is living through the Depression. We're a little short of cash right now for a purchase that large so I decided to harvest a few acres of timber myself to get the most money with the least land affected. We have enough timber on these 1200 acres that we can give up some for a special wedding present, even if Em doesn't like to see stumps. Besides she doesn't ride anymore and would rarely walk that far, so I figured she wouldn't have to see them anyway."

"How can you do that without talking to her? She told me she had sold you some land and then formed a partnership, but surely you have to discuss this kind of thing." Ann couldn't believe Em would consider it much of a gift to have her own timber cut without input in the decision.

"I won't go into the details of our partnership, but I don't need to talk to her, that's why she wasn't upset. The Forest Service knows I have the right to log or they wouldn't have given me the permit." He paused and looked at her with a slight tilt of his head and a hint of a smile. "I like the way you came out fighting for Em, even if you did spoil my surprise. You can check with the mill, when you get back. I'll tell them to give you whatever you need to feel more comfortable. But for now, how about a truce?"

Ann wasn't ready to give up her ideas about Ben yet. "I will talk to the mill," she confirmed, stiffly.

"Yes. Ma'am. It's a little early for anyone to be in. You'll need to wait. So, how do you like this place?" He asked, changing the subject.

"This little valley is incredible, like a mixing bowl with steep sides." She said, taking his hint to leave the battle for a while. "I haven't had much time to look around, but everything I've seen generates questions. Who lives here?"

"What kind of questions?"

"Why were the lights on if no one was here? I found a generator running now, but how, if it ran out a fuel last night?"

"The generator is on a timer, so it fires up at six each night and shuts down at nine. It fires up again at five in the morning and heats a little water for a shower, makes a pot of coffee too, if it's set up the night before."

"I'll bet it was the generator starting up that woke me up this morning," she replied. But the second the words were out of her mouth she wished she'd left sleeping out of the conversation.

He jumped right on it. "I saw the First Aid manual was on the couch. Did you use that for me last night? I know I wasn't any help and I don't remember a thing after we headed up the trail."

"Yes. I used it," she said helplessly feeling a blush spread uncontrollably over her cheeks and down her neck.

"Thanks," he answered, with a speculative glance at her coloring. "You probably saved my life despite what you think of me."

"Ben, I don't know what I think of you. I do, however, know how I feel about Em. I would fight anyone for her."

"Good. Em's worth it. I think this thing with the logging will clear itself up. So let's just talk about other things for now. This valley is, I believe, one of a kind."

Ann was starting to put things together. "This is your home, isn't it?"

"Yes, I built it, when I came back here after Henry died. Since then I've just been tinkering, adding little conveniences. I'll show you some while we do up breakfast."

In the kitchen he re-filled the coffee pot, explaining the system as he did. "The faucets here run from a tank in the attic. There is a very small electric hot water heater, so if you want a shower soon, you don't want to use the hot water faucet. I use the hand pump whenever it's convenient because regular use keeps it primed." Next he turned and pulled open a bin. It was filled with kindling. He explained that it was loaded from the back porch but could be reached quickly in the kitchen with this arrangement. A second bin tilted out to present somewhat larger pieces of wood to maintain the fire. As the stove warmed Ben continued explaining. "After you've used the range you can get hot water from this tank on the side. Just fill a pot and dump it in the sink for dishes, or whatever." He demonstrated using a spigot at the bottom of the tank. "After each use be sure to refill it with cold water so it won't go dry.

You regulate the heat of your cooking by moving the pans on the stove surface. Instead of changing a burner setting you use location for the different temperatures you want. On top of the fire chamber is high, in the center is medium or way over for low. You can also stick in a little more cedar kindling to get some fast heat. It takes a while to warm up, but this upper shelf is called bread warmer, and it's nice for keeping anything toasty. Come on out back and I'll show you the refrigerator."

Ben was obviously proud of his place and had no trouble putting more than three words together on this subject. When he was talking about his home made conveniences his enthusiasm showed through. The different sides of this man were fascinating. He not only sounded different, he looked different. He had on Dockers and a soft knit shirt that instead of lessening his rough masculinity, perversely highlighted it. The light brown against his tanned skin softened his face and his eyes lit up when he talked about his home. It was harder to imagine this man conning Em, although some of his innovations were probably expensive.

They went through the back porch, passed the compartment where she could hear the generator running, and out to the small building near the creek. Inside water ran from a pipe and splashed over some plastic bins in stair-stepped pools connected with little waterfalls. The pools were at different depths and had containers of different types. The stream that emanated from the pipe flowed across the small, heavily insulated room and out the other side. Ben started another commentary. "I decided to use a pipe to bring water from the creek since the level of the water there varies too much with each rain shower for easy management of the water level in the cooler. This way the pipe gives a constant flow. The room's thickened walls keep the temperature close to the water's year round. I've measured winter and summer; it stays between 40 and 50 degrees. The creek might freeze sometime in an unusual winter, I suppose, but it hasn't happened in the last ten years. The worst winters it gets a little ice on top but down below where the pipe get its feed it has always flowed. The water moves fast and in here it's protected by the building, so I think the risk of a solid freeze is small."

One by one he lifted baskets while giving instructions. "Always buy milk or juice in these plastic jugs with screw-on tops so they can set in the water, even waxed cardboard could soften. I keep the eggs in these plastic cartons so they won't get banged around. The lettuce or other perishables are in these Tupperware containers."

"How did you ever think of this?" Ann asked, ignoring but very aware of his implication that she might need to know how to buy groceries for these bins.

"Didn't really, just listened to Henry's stories of how they used to live before they had power. If I had a regular fridge, I'd have to run the generator all the time. It's fed from a small propane tank and it would be too much trouble getting all that gas in here."

"Do you carry everything in on horse back the way we came?"

"No, there's another way into the valley, I'll show you later."

Ann's mental picture of this man continued to shift. There was certainly much more to him than the simple ranch hand she had seen at first. That had many implications and she reminded herself to watch her step.

They took eggs and some bacon back inside. He readied some potatoes and put them and the meat on to cook, then excused himself and disappeared into the bedroom closing the door. Ann heard him mumbling to himself as she wandered around the small room.

She looked at the single painting on the wall, a nude woman with long black hair covering strategic spots. That fit. It was the kind of thing a lonely ranch hand might hang. But it was an unusual style. When he returned she asked him about the painting, expecting an answer that might be consistent with the original image she had of him.

"I bought it from an Indian fellow," he said, as he fried the eggs. "Here's the story he told me. She is Kawheelah, the daughter of an ancient chief and was the most beautiful woman anyone had ever seen. She was all any man could desire, but one day she went alone to bathe in the stream and never returned. She haunted the stream forever after. Sometimes a brave would go to the stream and see her as she is in that picture, wet from her bath, combing her long hair. From that moment on no other woman could satisfy him so he was destined to spend the rest of his life pining for another glimpse of her."

"Well, you can certainly glimpse plenty of her." She said nodding toward the painting.

"True. But that's not why it's there." He noted her skeptical look. "Damn. Don't get all Feminist on me. That picture means something to me."

"I'm sure."

"Not that. That story is how describes exactly how I feel. I saw the perfect woman in my mind, now no other will do. I can prove it. I wrote down what I pictured, I'll show you. Take this stuff to the table." Ann wasn't sure she wanted to know what he dreamed of, but took the food without comment.

He went to the bookcase, opened a box and brought back a piece of weathered graph paper covered with notes. He would eat a little then read a section thoughtfully. "'Sensitive: have felt pain but not despaired.' I think for man or woman the ability to go on is the key to a full life. We all get hit with hard blows. Some people absorb them and go on, others just give up. 'A lady: not a queen.' By that I mean she has to be willing to get her hands dirty sometimes. Not just physically around the barn, although that counts, but dig into serious issues even if they aren't straightforward and clean. There is one side note: not over five foot eight. Both my grandmother and mother were close to six foot tall. Grandmother worked her way up in the phone business. Redheaded, overbearing, guess she gave me most of my view of female bosses. I didn't like it. I wasn't able to look either of them in the eye until I was 17. I hated where we lived and a lot of other things. So I waged a constant war with them as I was growing up. I guess it really isn't height that bothers me; it's the battles. I don't want to live in that kind of turmoil again. I want a partner. Besides, I don't want to think about the trouble I gave them the last few years of their lives."

Ann couldn't help checking off in her mind. She had had her tough times after her parents died and now with the M.S., although he didn't know about that. She had stood up to the challenges pretty well, she believed. If she had been tested working around the barn, she would have passed. She might have gained some points trying to protect Em from a logging scam, even if it was aimed at him. She fit the height requirement.

He paused and gave her that off side smirk. She could see from his eyes that he had been watching her as the realization came over her, that she fit his 'standards'. She felt herself flare red as he nodded and continued. "'Not a young virgin: knowledgeable about life.' As I've gotten older I have felt that even more. I'm 48 now and too old to start a family. Besides I got myself into a long-term relationship several years back that we both agreed would not lead to marriage. I didn't want to take a chance on birth control or having a child, who like me, had no father. I had a vasectomy. I need a woman who has accepted not having a family."

Ann looked up at him. The revelations were coming a little too fast and too personal for her. Ben met her gaze, smiling softly. She felt a shiver. She didn't tell him that between her age and the M.S., she too felt that a family was out of the question, even if she found someone she cared about.

"After that relationship ended, I decided to focus all my efforts to this place and on helping Em. I was tired of the dating games and convinced if there was a woman out there for me, fate would bring her here. I stopped looking. I've been a much happier, healthier person since I came to that decision."

He didn't give her any chance to object to these confessions, or whatever he thought they were. She was still trying to figure out how to get them to something more neutral, when he turned the tables on her. "How about you? Have you settled on what kind of man you want?"

She raised her eyes and felt a flare of irritation. He knew he was flustering her and Ann was sure he was savoring every minute. She was not used to being confused, normally she controlled the situations around her quite easily. The annoyance was hard to hold on to. He looked so appealing with that little smile just playing at the corner of his mouth. He leaned toward her. She realized he was waiting for an answer but just shook her head.

The last few months, Ann had been fighting a loneliness that she hadn't allowed herself to feel for many years. First the M.S. diagnosis and then the disruption of her career had dredged up yearnings she thought she had firmly in control. Being with Em was helping in some ways but she wanted more. Right now she would settle for a man who wasn't scared off by the M.S. That was quite a shock to her since she had never just settled for anything in her life. The disease seemed to suck away a sex appeal she'd always taken for granted. She wanted to be held, loved and told everything would be all right. It flashed through her mind that Ben might be a candidate to fulfill that need. She had no intention of telling him anything like that though, so she remained silent.

After what felt like an eternity to Ann, Ben filled the heavy silence. "If you're not going to talk to me, then I'll just have to guess." Then he leaned back and looked her up and down like he was weighing his thoughts carefully and that close study of her might change the outcome. "You like a man who has a good income, is tall, with a good physique, nice straight teeth. You know the kind I mean, a pretty boy; the Greek God look."

"Thanks for giving me so much credit. Your want list for a woman scarcely touched on physical characteristics, but you assume that's all that's on my mind!" His remarks had hit her harder than she would like to admit, perhaps too close to home. She did usually date good-looking men. She had to admit she was raised to be a little class conscious but it was security that concerned her, not money. He took his time with his answer, still lazily resting back in his chair watching her closely.

"Well." He drawled with a little smile. "I saw you take to Dalton the first time you met, so it was a natural guess. Ran up to Seattle and stayed with him for a week. That must be the way they do it in the big city."

"How dare you judge me! It's none of you business, but I stayed in a hotel in Seattle, not with Dalton, that's how I do it in the big city. I don't jump in and out of the sack. As for taking to Dalton, start off with the fact that he's interesting and fun to talk to. He's intelligent and well read. He was thoughtful and offered to introduce me to Seattle, which will really help when I look for housing and a job. He's good at his profession, which means he makes a good living but it's not the only thing I care about. More than that, he was interested in me. That is a first criterion for a relationship. None of that has anything to do with his looks."

He didn't respond in any way to her indignation. Ann watched him sitting there apparently thinking through what she'd said. It occurred to her that he might be measuring himself against her standards. After a moment's thought she knew he wouldn't fit badly, now that she saw his library and he was suddenly willing to talk to her…except that she wasn't sure how horse breaking fit into the title of profession. She hadn't fit too badly into his arms this morning either, but she didn't want her mind to go any further that way.

Ben wasn't unhappy with her list. He fit them all, except that he didn't want to show her anywhere but here and she still wasn't aware that he was very interested in her. What's more he wasn't sure how she'd react when she found out. He leaned toward her with a satisfied look on his face. "Got you talking, didn't I?"

CHAPTER 9

Ann stood and started clearing the table. She felt a real need to get their conversation to safer ground. "Why do you grow that beard?"

"Why not?"

"It's unkempt."

"Look again. It's clean and neatly trimmed. You're just influenced by the old wives tale that women don't like beards. It's total prejudice, like the idea that all men like long hair on women."

"You don't like long hair?"

"Whatever a woman wants to do with her hair is O.K. by me. Long hair seems hard to care for. As for the beard, I usually only grow it in the fall and winter. It gets cold working outside in the rain and wind; the beard protects my face. I don't know why I have it this summer. Bet you've never known anyone with a beard and you think it's scratchy."

"That's true, I guess."

As they bantered back and forth Ben had readied the water and started on the dishes. Ann was glad they were talking about something superficial that didn't make her analyze her churning emotions.

"Why don't you try it?"

His words called her thoughts back. Ann reached up and self-consciously touched the beard. It was surprisingly soft.

"No, I mean give it a kiss. That's the only real beard test for a woman. Think of it as a way to expand your knowledge. It's on the house," he taunted her. "Won't cost you a thing." He turned his head, exposing his strongly muscled neck and offered his cheek.

Ann rose to the dare in his voice and stretched up to plant a peck on his fur-adorned jaw. He moved to meet her and their lips met. Ann felt fire course through her, but she pulled back.

"Two for the price of one. You're safe," he said, holding up some soapy dishes.

She didn't give herself a chance to think, slipping her hands around his neck and pulling his smirking lips to hers. She felt the wet suds covered hands against her back still filled with dishes, but she didn't care. When they finally broke, they stood there a minute trying to regain some composure. "We'd better talk," she said.

"That's what the old dining table is for." He replied, setting the dishes back in the sink. "Grampa said there was nothing that couldn't be discussed over his table and I've found that to be true."

"I'm not sure where to start. I came west largely because I was diagnosed with multiple sclerosis. That fact has so far ended a relationship in Chicago and another one here."

"I've known about the M.S. since before you arrived. Em wanted to do research so we'd know what would be good or bad for you. Not only have I read articles about the disease and its treatment, but I took Em to Olympia to a Support Group meeting."

Ann shivered. "I went to one of those. It scared me to death. Everyone there was using a walker or a wheelchair and they had trouble speaking. I think they were getting together to hear about treatments that might give hope. That's how they were keeping a good outlook. But for someone newly diagnosed like me, seeing the likely direction of the future wasn't a lot of support. It was terrifying."

"Maybe I had a little less personal involvement, or maybe just because it was a different group, what I saw was that only about half of the members needed some kind of device to help them move around. They tended to be either a lot younger or older than you. Like the literature says, a person has a better chance at a mild outcome if they are older when they contract the disease. Most people get the disease between 20 and 40. I believe that you were diagnosed at 38, right?" She nodded and he went on. "So with that in your favor and these new shots, you have every reason to be hopeful. That's not to say you won't face some challenges, but you've done that before."

"I didn't think I'd be able to give myself shots. When it came down to it though, I did it without hesitation. It's amazing how being scared let's you do just about anything."

"Not everyone reacts that way to fear. You've got some backbone. That's obvious from the way you took to riding and your defense of Em."

She didn't want to go back to that right now. "The other thing I hate is having needle tracks and injection site reactions. I carry a card with me in case a police officer should ever notice. I haven't been doing it for long so the issue of a bathing suit hasn't arisen. I think I'll just give up swimming. Shorts are even a concern. I got some longer walking shorts but still I have to be careful they don't pull up. Although around here there aren't that many days to worry about it," she said, trying to lighten the mood with a little humor. "You probably think I'm being a little superficial. I feel that way, but I can't stop it from bothering me. I care about the way I look."

"Ann, it's like the issue with long hair. The long hair itself can be eye catching, but it's the woman who's appealing. Little things like a red spot on the skin don't even come into the equation. Well, unless…I mean…are the injection sites sore?"

"No. Just ugly sometimes, not always."

Ben switched them to another issue. "As for your experience with Dalton, you weren't really fair to him, holding the M.S. information back. Although I'm sure it's a little hard to fit into a conversation. As you said, he's a thoughtful man, even if I find him obnoxious some-times. Half his panic was over literally forcing you up that hill."

"How do you know about that?" She couldn't imagine Dalton had told him about her dragging herself down the hill on a stick. She doubted he would tell anyone that he just stood there and stared.

"Oh. Dalton and I square off all the time, but whenever he gets into trouble he runs right here. He doesn't have a brother, and nei-ther do I. We fight like siblings so we might as well have some of the positive side too. We both hung out here with Em & Henry since we were kids."

"So, what did he tell you?"

"Dalton was sick about what happened and not sure what to do next. He doesn't have your strength when he's afraid. But there are other concerns."

"What do you mean?"

"He might have gotten over his shock and come back around if you had some other disease. But uncertainty really throws Dalton off track and the idea of M. S. terrifies him. He likes things organized so he has planned his life well ahead. He was already concerned that, although he really liked you, you didn't seem to fit with his plans. He just hoped you two might be able to work things out. A big hurdle in his mind was your age. You're past the prime child bearing years and the M.S. just capped things."

Ann interrupted. Her instant anger wouldn't let her sit still. "Child bearing! Is he looking for a woman or a brood mare?"

"Easy girl. It's not personal with him. He's been working on his life blueprint for a lot of years now. He laid out a schedule: first law school, establish credentials, move back to Washington, marriage, 2.5 children and grand things from there. He has political ambitions and you don't fit into that mold very smoothly. But there are bigger issues than that, although I'm sure he doesn't know it."

"What could be bigger than potentially being bound to a woman in a wheel chair or worse?" She responded, her bitterness coming through.

"I think being tied to the wrong woman would be much worse. He thought you were the woman for him because you're independent and successful. That, he felt, would make you the perfect partner for a man with ambitions. I mostly let him ramble, but the fact is I've heard him say almost those same words more than once when he came to cry in his beer over other lost loves. He thinks he wants a self-sufficient woman, until the first time her career conflicts with his. If she doesn't put his needs and goals first, that's the beginning of the end.

There's another thing. You command a healthy salary. If it topped Dalton's, I don't think he could handle it. That boy has a lot of ego."

Whereas a con man on the prowl would never be put off by extra money, she cynically told herself. But she was surprised Ben had even observed Dalton's chauvinistic tendencies. "So what did you advise him?"

"I told him not to worry. You wouldn't hate him, but you aren't the right woman for him."

"That's taking a lot on yourself. How do you know that?"

"He is too oriented to the politics of any situation. You can tell by his clothes and apartment. They are more oriented to the right look than personal comfort.

Besides, I believe there is a better man for you." He went on before she could follow that up. "The reason I understand the problem of fitting difficult personal news into a conversation is that I've been facing that for years. I'm a recovering alcoholic. I've been dry for 10 years, but still it's a problem I'll always live with. I don't know what all that booze and being slammed around on a bull did to my insides but I'm sure it hasn't added to my longevity. Now, I think we've had enough talk for a while." He stood, took both her hands and pulled her up after him.

She couldn't remember talking to anyone this frankly. Far from being a man who couldn't put three words together, he had drawn her feelings out and seemed to understand her, maybe more than she did herself. She felt a strong physical attraction to him, too. It had been there all along but she had consciously put it aside. A fling with the hired help wasn't her idea of a good thing to do. Well, he wasn't exactly hired help but still she knew if her mother was alive that's the way she would look at him. It was a part of her upbringing. She just didn't want that kind of complication in her life right now. She looked up and found he was studying her thoughtfully.

Ben didn't want to push too fast and have Ann run scared. On the other hand she was no 20-year-old virgin. She was a strong woman who knew what she wanted, maybe thrown off just a little by the M.S. Still she had certainly responded to him in the kitchen. He felt she was ready to move along. He was more than ready, having brooded over her for a couple of months. He pulled her slowly into his embrace. She didn't give him any negative signals, so he kissed her thoroughly.

Ann couldn't remember a kiss that made her feel this alive. There was something about this man. His lack of concern with convention made him intriguing. But it was his lean strength that sent shivers through her as he molded their bodies together. Since she'd obviously responded to his advance, she expected that kiss to lead to some maneuvering toward the bedroom, and wasn't sure she would object. While she usually liked to start relationships off slowly, this one seemed to be unusual in many ways.

Ben caught her totally off guard. He suddenly released her and stepped back. She was surprised to see him smiling from ear to ear. "Do you know it's afternoon already?" He said. "It's supposed to get to 75 degrees today in town, a real change from yesterday. With no wind here in the valley it will be 80 and we need to take advantage of the good days when we get them around here. He headed into the back, came out with a couple of towels and motioned toward the back door."

"Wait," she said. "I need to get back. For one thing, I need to go pick up the refill on my prescription."

After a moment's thought he returned to the bedroom and she could hear his voice.

"You have a phone." She accused him when he returned.

"Yes. I didn't know there was anything wrong with that."

"There isn't. It's just that I sure would have liked to have known that last night."

"It's in a wooden box on the far side of the bed. I put it in so Em could call if she needs anything. Anyway, the prescription's all taken care of. Bronco will pick it up. You don't need a shot til tomorrow. Right?" She nodded acknowledgment. He went on responding to her frowning expression. "Bronco likes to tell stories, but he keeps confidences. Besides he wouldn't say anything embarrassing. He likes you and your skills at chicken coop cleaning. Besides, he already knew you were here. I called him earlier so he wouldn't worry when he saw your horse was gone."

Ben took her hand, led her out the back, into the field and along the creek. The trail was easy walking through knee high grass. The water they followed upstream was running fast with banks a foot high. After about 30 yards there were large rocks partially blocking the flow. Behind them in a sweeping bend the water widened out and formed a deep pool. "It's cold, but it feels wonderful and this spot is just deep enough for a nice swim."

"I don't have a suit and I don't skinny dip."

"You didn't really tell all, but my senses tell me this won't be the closest we've been today. Skinny-dipping will wait but it is a great experience you should try some time. If you dive, dive shallow until you know the bottom well." Ben stripped to his shorts dove cleanly into the pond.

He was right. It was a little silly to be prissy now. She turned her back, stripped down to panties and bra and quickly stepped to the water's edge. She planned to follow his lead with a speedy entry, but just the touch of the water left her chilled. She remembered what he'd said about a constant 50 degrees.

Ben appraised her as she stood there and she felt herself flush again as his eyes traveled over her body. This time it started at the roots of her hair and spread with an unrelenting tingle to her toes. She was angry at her inability to conceal how he affected her. She was very conscious their discussion about the red blotches on her thighs and stomach. She knew he saw them but she didn't see anything but approval in his eyes. He swam toward her and when the water was too shallow, he stood.

The site of his glistening body eclipsed all thoughts about herself. She felt a thrill of excitement and goose bumps from more than the cold water tickling her toes. She suddenly realized that the flimsy underclothes she was wearing made her reaction obvious to his roving gaze and she dove in.

Ben returned to the creek, they swam together for a few minutes; then he urged her out of the water. Shivering violently, they walked up the bank where Ben picked up the towels and led the way into the surrounding grass. There was an area where the grass was flattened in a circular pattern. Ben used the spot to lay out one of the over sized towels. Giving a wave of his hand that she assumed meant for her to lay down. Ann followed his direction and stretched out on her stomach, feeling more secure that way.

He knelt beside her. "We wouldn't want any more hypothermia." He joked as he took the corner of the other towel and teasingly wiped at each drop on her back.

"Stop tickling, that's not helping!"

"Yes, Ma'am." The towel left and was replaced by his lips and tongue moving from drop to drop. He started at her shoulders and slowly worked down. His beard made a soft pattern on her skin as he moved. She tensed slightly as the bra came loose and he worked lower. Then she felt just the beard as he teasingly moved back up along her spine. His hand reached for her shoulder, turned her over and kissed her deeply. That warmed her and the shivering stopped. She was still on edge, not sure what she felt. He pulled back only slightly. His lips were close to hers, his voice husky with desire. "Just say stop and I will, but don't play with me. I will stop." He paused for only a second more, she couldn't reply. She just held her breath, until once again his lips began moving down from her neck to her shoulder.

Desire surged through her. But, she knew what came next, he would start groping her breasts. She was ready for that typical move and would feel somehow justified in calling a stop to his explorations. This was crazy. Things were moving too fast. But the lips moved so excruciatingly slow; on her shoulder down her collarbone with infinite tenderness. He was savoring every inch of her and it felt incredible. He reached that little valley between her breasts blocked by any further movement by the bra. By then she knew what she wanted. "Don't stop." She whispered. Ben had no problem following that instruction.

He pulled the interfering fabric away. His strong hand found one breast enclosing it while his mouth covered the other. She arched toward him. Her hand reached for his hardened member. He pulled back and retrieved her hand kissing it gently. "I'm in charge this time." He said. "I don't think I could take much touching there right now." As he said this he removed his shorts, pulled the obligatory plastic package seemingly out of nowhere. When he was ready he pressed himself tightly against her. Then his lips were back, her one hand firmly entrapped by his strong grasp. She used the other to encircle the back of his head and press his mouth into her breast. He concentrated his attentions on first one then the other. When they had hardened to the point they felt they might burst, he moved his kisses slowly down. He teased her stomach. The notion briefly ran through her mind that he was kissing her blotchy injection sites. But that thought fled as he moved down to the top of her panties.

Once again almost of its own volition her body bowed toward him. He took advantage of her lifting hips to move the enclosing fabric away. She trembled. He just kept licking, kissing, nipping at her,across her hips and down her thigh. By this time any concerns about little imperfections on her body were long gone. He started back up her other leg. As he reached her inner thigh she wasn't sure what to expect and her muscles tightened. He just continued up to tease her stomach again. She went limp with unanticipated disappointment and then his hand was there, where her desire was focused. The magic fingers brought her higher and higher. Soon every inch of her body stiffened as the ecstasy flooded through her. The fingers didn't stop. Her body felt ablaze.

Then he was inside her, holding down both of her arms as he thrust into her. Being trapped from even touching him enflamed her further. She rebelled the only way she could against her imprisonment, meeting his every thrust with a fierce lunge of her own. The heat raced through her again and that was all it took for him. He joined her in the explosion.

After they'd both come back to earth, he held them tightly together and rolled to his back. Keeping her close he said, "That was everything I dreamed of and more, my Kawheelah." They drifted off together in the warm afternoon sun.

They awoke comfortably snuggled in each other's arms. Ann's eyes slowly drifted, focusing on the grass around them. "What are those?" She asked, looking at some small oval faded brown pebbles.

"That's elk sign."

"You mean dung?"

"Shit. Yes, that's what I mean. You can add to your autobiography that you screwed in an elk bed, that's what that little grass circle was. Isn't that the sort of thing fantasies are made of?"

"I don't fantasize. Besides there aren't any elk here."

"You should try a little day dreaming, it's great relaxation. We can work on that later." He chuckled. "Look at that broken shale slope on the far side of the valley. The elk come down that slide every fall to rut and hide out during hunting season. I sometimes hunt but never here. Our land is posted No Hunting and the elk are safe here. They've been gone for months, that's why the pellets are so faded out."

He slipped his arm out from under her and jumped up, pulling her up after him. "Well, we sure got you out of your gloomy mood and your mind on something more fun than trees. Now let's try that skinny dipping." He teasingly patted her bottom and headed away.

She was left standing nude in the middle of the valley and was totally amazed at herself. In her urban world, there were people everywhere. Sex was something you did under the covers in the privacy of your bed. She had never experienced anything this open and free, to say nothing of this explosive. On the other hand that last remark jarred her deeply. Reminded of Em and her timber, she wondered how she had ever let herself get this distracted. She had to keep her head for her aunt's sake. It was obvious Ben had planned this event from pretty early on in the day from his comments. She was running a little behind…not thinking straight. He was good, very slick; no wonder he had been able to take in Em. I was a total fool to think I'd suddenly found someone who saw past the M.S. He could see how desperate I've felt since that scene with Dalton. All it took was a little pity F___ (I hate that word I won't even think it) and he thought I'd just forget and forgive everything. No matter whether I'm attracted to him, I owe it to Em not to get sucked in. She walked resolutely after Ben.

CHAPTER 10

Ann dove into the creek. This time more than the water chilled her. When they got out and dressed Ben was ebullient, but she didn't listen to anything he was saying. She just wanted to get back to the house. The sooner she set off for Seattle the better. She needed to get away from him quickly before she completely lost hold of her better judgment. She would check with the mill as a starter. But she had to assume Ben would talk to them first, so she couldn't end it there. Who knows what he might tell them to get their cooperation. He had easily fooled the Forest Service and this was a small town. She would then head up to the city as she planned and stay there until she was sure Em and Hal had returned. Maybe a talk with Hal would be her next step.

She finally tuned back in to what Ben was saying. "Tomorrow I have a place I'd love to show you. I think…"

"Stop right there," she interrupted. "You're making assumptions. I am not staying another night."

"Oh. Well, we can run down and get whatever you need and be back in an hour." He advanced toward her, his arms reaching out. Ann moved back quickly. He stopped with a puzzled look.

"The fact that we rolled around in some dead grass doesn't change a thing. I still have every intention to check with the mill. You didn't distract me, if that's what you think, with a quick bang for the sick girl."

His jaw clenched and his face paled as he stepped back like he'd been slapped. "That's what it meant to you? I guess you really don't think much of yourself. I gave you way too much credit for guts. Honey, when I'm giving out pity fucks I send engraved invitations!

As for checking with the mill, go! Go anywhere but here, I could care less. Pick up anything you left in the house. I'll saddle Comanche." He grabbed his shirt, turned and tried to stomp away but it was obviously painful and his limp increased as he went.

Ann's stomach was turning over. She wanted to take everything back, to reach out and kiss that look off his face. Men like Ben weren't supposed to react like this. He had really looked hurt. Watching him was torture but she held back, forcing herself to think of Em. She just slowly finished dressing and went back to the cabin. She picked up her rain gear on the back porch and peaked timidly in but didn't see or hear Ben. When she came out of the house, he was nowhere in sight. Comanche was saddled out front, standing hip shot, waiting for her. They rode out of the valley, for the last time she was sure.

When Ann arrived at The Homestead, Bronco came out of the barn. He looked surprised. "Where's Ben?"

"He's up at his cabin, where he belongs." She replied and led her horse inside before there were any other questions. For all she knew he could be part of this scheme. Besides she couldn't talk about Ben right now. The last look she'd had of his face was burning too freshly in her mind.

At the house, Ann changed and took her luggage to the car. She found her new prescription in the fridge. She packed it carefully into a cool-pack, added the needles she'd need. She would stop at the mill on the way out of town. "I need to get this over and done with," she said though there was no one to hear it. She didn't express, even for her own ear the rest of the thought; "before I chicken out." She really dreaded having her judgment of Ben confirmed. She quickly drove away.

The man who met her at the door was late middle aged. He looked work hardened and tired but he greeted her with a huge welcoming grin. "Hi. I've seen you around with Em. You're Ann, right?."

"Yes. I'm glad you know who I am because I'd like to ask you for some of Em's records of recent logging sales. I know it's a little unusual…"

"Heck. Ben asked me to keep these scale receipts here so Em wouldn't see them. I think it's great if you take them. This stuff just gets in the way around here. That Ben's something else isn't he? Haven't seen such a hard working cuss in a long time. Gutsy, too, working that logging show alone, but that's giving him plenty of cash for the motor home. I know Hal was more than pleased. Last Lion's Club meeting he was going on and on about how he planned to stop on this trip with Em at a factory in Oregon that Ben had investigated. That's how Hal's going to break the surprise to her, just pull up into the showroom. If they have one on hand Hal and Em like, they just might come back driving the thing and towing the car. Ben put the money he has so far in a joint account so they could just buy one if they want. Price of timber's up right now and I'm sure he'll have the rest of the money in there soon. Now me, I'd have broken the good news to her myself, but that's not Ben's way. Hal gets all the fun. Well, here are your statements."

"Everybody in town knows?" She choked out.

"Sure. There aren't many secrets around here. Besides, we all want to be a part. For wedding gifts, you know. Doris, my wife, is a little organizer. Case you didn't notice, I'm the gabber; she's the planner. Anyway she has people signing up for: sheets, towels, dishes, stainless, utensils. Hal promised to bring back fabric samples because Doris wants everything to coordinate. They'll get everything they need for their new toy. Otherwise it's hard to find anything for a gift that folks can use with their years of accumulation. Doris was going to call you to see if you wanted to sign up, but she was worried Em would answer. Anyway she figured you might already have a gift in mind, maybe worked something out talking to Ben."

Ann took the slips of paper he thrust toward her, without a word and bolted from the office. She drove hastily back to The Homestead. She wasn't sure what to do next. Her head spun from the realization of how her stubborn refusal to listen to Em or Ben caused her to act like a real idiot.

When she entered the house, she noticed the message light was blinking. It was for her, from Pam Rausch. She wanted a return call right away. Said it was urgent. It was the last thing she cared about right now but…

Pam answered on the first ring. She was relieved to hear Ann's voice. Twice a man named Terry Johnson had called on Pam, he wanted to be Ann's agent. He would distribute her artwork through several outlets around the state. One of the places he represented, Pam told her excitedly, was 'Washington's Bounty'. Ann hadn't heard of it. Pam explained it was a retail store, doing very well with a number of shops in, for example, the airport and Seattle Center. It could be very profitable to have her artwork there. Pam wanted to arrange for Ann to meet Terry as soon as possible.

"Pam," she said, "I consider you my agent. I wouldn't have gotten into this at all without you. Please handle everything for me. We've worked out a 20 percent split for you, offer him another 10 or whatever you think is right."

"Let's start with 5%," Pam responded promptly. "Honestly though, I can lower my percentage of whatever is sold outside my store. He's talking about some up front investment to get the first round of copies made."

"That would be hard for me, right now. Offer him a higher percentage, I think, and try to talk him out of any cash."

"I doubt I can do that. But, I believe in this, Ann. I would be willing to invest in you. Only thing is, if we get into 'Washington's Bounty,' you can't move out of the state."

"That's not a problem. I'll be staying on."

They went on quickly to make arrangements for a meeting the next week to go through more of her sketches and select those that should be finished first. Pam let Ann know there would probably be deadlines to get her art ready and was assured there would be no problem.

Now, Ann had no excuses left. She needed to face her issue with Ben. She wandered in the kitchen and began almost unconsciously preparing coffee. It was easier to think things through with a cup in her hand. He had been telling her the truth all along. She had just ignored what he said and thought the worst of him. To be honest she'd enjoyed the role of Em's protector too much to let it be taken away.

She took another sip and almost choked on it. She had let her ego get in the way, not wanting to admit she was wrong. But now, focusing on her embarrassment, she was almost missing the real point. If he wasn't lying about Em, then everything he did and said at the cabin and by the creek was real! She'd met a man who didn't care about her diagnosis. On top of that she found him terribly attractive, almost against her will. She had really enjoyed talking to him and the creek bank...Wow! And with all that going for her, she'd slapped him down. She was more than a self-centered brat, sne was crazy and throwing away everything she'd been searching for. She had to get back to the valley. She had to try to make Ben understand how sorry she was, how torn she been.

As she hurried to get her riding clothes, she was really feeling the fatigue that the stress and excitement brought on. Walking was a challenge and she was glad that Comanche would do all the work of getting back to the valley. To conserve energy, she drove her car down and around the barn. Bronco's truck was gone, so there was one explanation avoided. She managed to saddle Comanche. She borrowed some saddlebags from the wall, tucked in her medicine for tomorrow; just in case. Then she quickly mounted and rode away. The trip to Ben's cabin seemed to take forever. Still she hadn't decided what to say to him. Maybe the words would come to her when she saw him.

Ann's dread of facing Ben was tempered only slightly by the good news from Pam. It could mean she might support herself without going to Seattle or at least work only part time out of town. The ad layouts might continue to grow, too. If she could just straighten things out with Ben…

Ann rode Comanche direct to the barn, unsaddled him and turned him out with Peanut. She saw no sign of Ben but she heard Merle Haggard playing loudly in the cabin. She threw her saddlebag over her shoulder, walked to the cabin and up the back steps with trepidation. She opened the door without knocking. Ben and Bronco were sitting at the table. There was an ice bucket and in the center of the table an open bottle. Each of the men had a raised glass. They seemed to be drinking a toast. She froze, remembering what he'd said about being a recovering alcoholic.

They had heard the door open and turned. Bronco started to sputter out something but Ben stopped him. "I don't owe her any kind of explanation." He addressed Ann. "Forget something?"

"Yes. I'm seven kinds of a fool. I forgot what it's like to trust. I forgot to listen with my heart and not my cynical mind. I came back to crawl, to beg if I have to and see if we could try again but…"

"But what? Bronco and I are spending an afternoon together."

"The bottle; you said…"

"I said I don't drink alcohol anymore."

She stopped and thought about why she had returned here. She came to tell him she should have trusted him. Now what was she doing? She took a deep breath. "It just looks like you're drinking. Tell me you're not and I'll believe you."

"Despite all the evidence?"

It was the hardest answer she could ever remember being asked to give. The facts were there for anyone to see. "Yes," she whispered.

"That didn't sound too convincing."

"Trusting is a hard chore for me, I'll admit." She told him with more conviction. "But I'm sure about this."

"O.K. I'm not drinking."

Ann started to approach Ben but he waved her to the couch and moved to a chair across the room. He had no intention of letting her smell his breath to bolster her conviction. He wanted to know she meant it. On the other hand, Bronco had just been climbing all over him. He had been the fool not to talk to her frankly about the partnership and even take her to the mill before he tried to change things between them. He was too eager and he knew it. He'd been bemoaning his idiocy to Bronco when she came in. On the other hand, he was still hurting a bit from the rejection. That offer to beg was a little too good to pass up. "So you went to the mill." He declared. She nodded. "Are you still headed for Seattle? Or are you spending the night?"

She remembered the saddlebag and flashed an embarrassed glance at Bronco. She saw the smirk she expected. This was a test and she was ready. "I'll stay, if I'm invited."

"O.K. Bronco, we need some time alone."

Bronco shrugged. "Two more stubborn, I ain't never seen." He left.

They were silent for a few minutes, before Ben set the tone. "I don't think we can take up very comfortably where we left off." His teasing smile went a long way toward relaxing Ann. "What say we just talk?"

"How did Bronco end up here?"

"He kept me out of trouble when I joined the circuit. He spotted my problem and sponsored me into A. A. I owe him a lot. He was too old to hang around the rodeo anymore, so when I left I just convinced him we could use him here."

"You mean like Fiero'; a comfortable retirement?"

"Something like that." He agreed, but moved their conversation in a new direction. "Let me give you a little history on this valley. I loved to wander through the woods as a kid. One day I followed an animal trail into this valley and fell in love with it. It was my place and I spent every free minute here. I told Henry about it. He knew his neighbor was trying to sell his land and talked him into separating out this ¼ section. Since it had no timber and was so hard to get to, the guy found it pretty worthless and Henry got it for a steal. Anyway, I worked for him and paid him back. It's how I learned to log. The place has been mine for a long time. The challenge of making it comfortable here is what kept me going. Now I've been thinking about you and this Seattle thing."

Ann interrupted him. "Ben, I might not need to be in Seattle as often as I planned." She told him with a glow about her plans to meet with the buyer and Pam Rausch the following week.

"Now that calls for congratulations. Come here." He rose to meet her with a crushing embrace. They were lost for some time in the wonder of being back in each other's arms. They had been so close to losing what had only begun to bloom. The thought made them cling to each other fiercely.

"Whew". Ann sighed. "Unless you want to retire without dinner, I suggest we start working on a little distraction."

"You're hungry?"

"Actually, yes. No lunch, remember?"

"Yes. Ma'am." He said and headed toward the kitchen.

"Why do you do that, 'yes ma'am' stuff? It's out of character and part of the reason I decided you worked for Em."

"It's my way of dealing with a strong willed woman, who has obviously made up her mind. It's kept me out of harms way for a long time." He said with a belly laugh, as she playfully pummeled him.

"You can clear that old bottle off the table. It goes in this cupboard. Bronco brings the ice and steaks. I supply the cola and fixing's when we have a pity party. The empty bottle is to collect up any rotten memories. It's a tradition we started way back when I quit drinking, facing the bottle literally. Anyway, we won't need it any more tonight."

They dined on steaks courtesy of Bronco, bar-b-cued over a portable propane grill. Dinner was fixed and eaten with inconsequential banter and only an occasionally wandering hand.

It was still light when they went to the barn and climbed into the loft. Ann rested as Ben forked fresh straw into the stalls. "Is that for Fiero?" She asked.

"Sure is. He loves it here about as much as I do. He's turned into quite a puppy. Still he's one you should never trust too far. He had a lot of years of hard treatment and can be a little unpredictable."

When Ben was done Ann jumped up. She hurried toward the ladder calling, "Ladies first. I want to watch your tight jeans as you come down."

"Oh no you don't." He grabbed her around the waist and twirled her out of the way. "Ladies are never first on a ladder. That's a man's prerogative. Besides your pants are tighter."

Things progressed rapidly from there.

Later Ann let him know, "This rolling in the hay isn't all it's cracked up to be in novels. It pokes and itches." She hopped up, dressed and beat him to the ladder. From below she teased him, "Put a little more wiggle in it!" He growled and jumped, landing on his already damaged ankle.

"That should teach me," he said as she helped him up to head back to the cabin and his cane, "to act like I'm a kid! On the other hand, it's how I feel. I'd given up on ever feeling like this. I guess that's when the old man up stairs makes it happen. You know, when you stop looking, relax and accept."

"Maybe so. I hadn't admitted to myself that I'd given up. On the other hand, I've come to expect that things would fall apart. I believed deep down that the M.S. would cause any sensible person to run."

"Could be, but then no one's ever accused me of having much sense."

Ann tightened her grip around his waist as they walked.

At the cabin they begin to talk again. They couldn't seem to learn enough about each other. As they sipped a final cup of coffee, he opened up a little on his finances. "The money I used to help Em out with the mortgage was not all from horse training and rodeo work. My grandparents both worked for AT&T and accumulated quite a bit of stock through company stock plans. When they and Mom died in a boating accident, I inherited all of it. The Feds split the 'Ma Bell' phone company into the 'Baby Bells' and they've sure been growing. My holdings have pretty well skyrocketed. That stock kind of got me interested in the market. I sold some and diversified a little. I bought a few shares of other stuff. One was a local company that's done pretty well."

She noted the smirk on his face when he said that. An idea stuck her. "Microsoft?"

He nodded and went on. "Kind of too bad I had to sell all of that to save Em's land, I could be rolling in it now. I still have plenty of dividends from the phone stuff. I only logged the timber because the motor home was a large, unexpected expense. Otherwise the saddle training and dividends take care of what Em and I need." Ben was watching Ann closely, while he talked about money. It was something he'd never been very comfortable with. He had spent a lot of years keeping a closed mouth about it. The men he knew on the rodeo circuit couldn't stand people with money. Bronco was one of the most outspoken. Keeping his finances private had become a real habit. Still, he'd learned today that Bronco knew a lot more about his finances than he'd expected. He'd really chewed Ben for not being more open with Ann. Now he was trying but...

Ann wanted to get him off the subject of money. She didn't feel the need for the details of his income. She fully intended to support herself, no matter where this relationship went. It did help her to see how Ben had accomplished so much in the valley, but it made her uncomfortable. She thought about what he'd just said and jumped to change the direction of their conversation.

"Why do you call it saddle training? I've never heard it described that way before. I've watched you working with the horses. You do it differently than I expected. Have you studied that 'horse whispering' thing that's getting so much publicity? There are books out and there was even a movie."

"I don't call it breaking because I don't. I like horses," he said, (The corners of his mouth turned up for just a second, if she had blinked she would have missed it.) "and women with spirit. So I just work on trust. They will usually partner up with me and let me ride. I charge based on the age and experience of the rider and the horse's temperament. Parents around here know that if the horse isn't right for their kid, I'll tell them. Em just notes the fees, acts as banker and collector.

I've always treated horses this way. Most riders I've known who aren't in a rodeo do. I sure don't whisper, that's just a term they use, not what anyone who knows horses would do. It sounds like a hissing snake and that's sure to spook a horse. Em bought me those books as a little joke when they came out. It's interesting the stir they're raising but I've just found that horses are afraid of anything new and different. I get them used to my voice. I put the riding paraphernalia around so they can smell it and see it. That's half the battle when you first try to saddle them. Besides I take it real slow. I've had a little trouble getting my timing right with you. I was so slow Dalton almost cut in. Then I moved so fast I didn't clean up this thing with the logging."

She struck a haughty pose. "Do you always plan your strategies with women like you do with horses?"

"Well, sure. A filly is a filly!" The smile flashed again.

Ann continued. "You certainly are talkative all of a sudden. I didn't think that you put more than three words together, unless you were communing with a horse."

"People talk too much. I'd much rather be with someone who senses what I'm thinking or needing." He paused and she thought about how often when they worked he just looked at something or made a quick hand signal. She looked at him now and he nodded, another silent communication. "I've talked more today because I have things to say and I figured I had one chance. From the moment I woke up this morning, I planned to have you understand a lot more about me before you left here. I want to know more about you, too."

"O.K. But I don't know where to start."

"How about when you first found yourself on your own? How did you keep going?"

"Well, for one thing, I haven't ever gotten over the feelings of loss I had when my parents were suddenly gone and I had nothing. I vowed then never to go through that again, never to be financially dependent on someone else. Security is my strongest motivator. I need to make my own way and I get a lot of satisfaction out of it, too." She could see his reluctant acceptance.

"Since I started having problems with the M.S., it's been the little things that have bothered me most. I'm not used to seeing myself limited in any way. Like the loft. I love it, but I'm nervous about the stairs. Especially coming down, I hate the uncertain feeling it gives me and the knowledge that I may soon have quit going up there."

Ben didn't comment. He and Bronco had been working on a way around those stairs. They'd finalized things that morning, even though he wasn't sure whether Ann would be staying at The Homestead much longer. It would be nice for Em, too. They had agreed on how to have it completed. It should be done tomorrow. He regretted not taking care of it sooner, but said nothing to Ann about his plans.

CHAPTER 11

As they started talking about the homestead, Ann said the terrain sometimes still confused her. "That," Ben said, "is just because you haven't seen an overall view. Once you've really looked at a map it will all come clear." Ben enthusiastically pulled some graph paper, sophisticated looking pencil and a scaled ruler out of a drawer.

"An engineering left over?"

"Maps and lists! I never have enough. Besides I often like to draw things up before I start into a project." Ben started laying out a map. He explained the different symbols and shades he was using and Ann made notes for herself.

As he marked in the old-growth area, Ben paused. "I know Dalton took you into this patch of timber. I saw your tracks. I'm glad you've seen it, but next time; walk. Dalton knows I keep the horses and beef fenced out of there. Domestic animals stir up the soft ground and moss too much and cut deep paths. You've seen the difference between beaten down stock trails and deer paths that disappear if you don't keep a close watch. Are animals are too much creatures of habit and would want well-defined paths besides the additional foliage they would eat. The old growth should be preserved in every way. I feel a peace in there that's indescribable."

"Sorry, I didn't know. I'd love to go back. It was wonderful. I'd heard of old growth but I never imagined it would be so different. I'd like to take my sketch book next time."

He hesitated for a moment. "I took a woman there once. I thought I loved her, even thought I might propose there. She hated it! Said it felt evil and brooding. That was the beginning of the end. Anyway I'd really like to go back there with you." Then he quickly continued with the drawing and explanations, although a sort of awkward feeling lingered as they both digested what he'd said.

"What will happen to this place when you're gone? I mean, since you won't have children."

Ben eagerly jumped at the change of topic. "I've thought a lot about that over the years and focused on a couple options. First, I had this hair-brained idea to get the politicians to declare this a wilderness area. When I was younger that sounded very idealistic. As the years went by I watched the political shenanigans it takes to get land designated that way. Then too, I've seen what happens to the wilderness areas. They draw hikers like a magnet. Areas that have been left undisturbed since time began seem ideal for wilderness designation, but once they get marked that way on a map every hiker knows JUST where to go and they're never the same. Since this area would be so small, and close to a county road, it would be overrun.

So the idea I settled on was to donate this valley and old growth to a university. The cabin could be used to house students. They could hike down to the old growth or study the plants and animals around here. The valley is unusual with its natural grasses. Anyway, some time ago I did some preliminary investigation on that. I talked to the University of Washington first. They were sort of lukewarm on the idea, not sure if they wanted the maintenance responsibility. When I talked to Evergreen College though, you know they have a much more open approach to education, they nearly drooled."

"What's to stop them from logging it and taking the money, as soon as it's turned over?"

"That's easy. The papers will say that the college has perpetual use. But if it's ever decided to log, the land and proceeds go to the Children's Home Society. There's nothing a bureaucrat hates more than giving something away. So I think they'll find innovative uses. Might have to convert the barn into a bunkhouse or something."

"Sounds like it will work. So have you talked with Em on the old growth? That's part of The Homestead from the map. I always believed that Em would want to leave this place to her family. She has lots of nieces and nephews on her side that she's close to. She's always talking about them."

Ben paused and seemed to be formulating how to word his answer. "Em has never shown me her will, but she does love those kids and will certainly leave most of her holdings to them." He gave her a sideways look. "The old-growth will go with the bowl." He stated firmly. Ann sensed that was all he had to say on that subject. She wasn't sure if she had touched a nerve talking about Em passing or if he was sensitive to not having a real blood tie to Em anymore than she did.

When they finally were too tired to keep talking and filling each other with everything they could about themselves, they went toward the bedroom. It seemed silly after their escapades on the creek bank and the hay, but they felt somewhat shy. Maybe, it was the feeling that this was the start of a relationship on a different plane. Their lovemaking was passionate, but tender. It much more normal—in a bed and under the covers.

In the morning they conserved hot water with a shower for two. While Ann gave herself an injection, Ben prepared a quick breakfast of oatmeal and started to discuss his plans for the day until she slowed him down. This wasn't a living arrangement that could just suddenly happen. They had a few more days before Em returned but she should go back for some clothes.

"Yes, Ma'am. But let's be together for right now. Em is gone and you made arrangements with everyone else to be in Seattle. Stay another day."

"I need a change of clothes, at least."

"Jeans are good for a week! I'll get you a fresh shirt. Today there's a place I want to show you. It won't be easy, but I've given it a lot of thought. It won't be like it was with Dalton, even though you do need to hike. The trail is wide enough most of the way. There is one bad place but I've put up a rope for security. Just trust me to take good care of you." She nodded her agreement.

Ben went to the bedroom and returned with a shirt, some light-hiking boots that laced up over the ankles and another cane. The boots were her size "Either you have a shoe store in there or you have thought about this."

"I have to admit sneaking a visit to the loft a while back to make sure I got the right size. I won't pretend I haven't been dreaming about showing you my valley. You put these on; they'll help steady you. They have a lot of ankle support. I'll pack a few things."

He busied himself in the kitchen and bedroom for a few minutes. When he returned he had what appeared to be a full daypack. "Now let me show you the difference between the cane and the walking stick you improvised with Dalton. The walking stick is a lot heavier; it has to be lifted ahead of you with an upraised arm. It can be very tiring. With the cane, we'll adjust it so it is like an extension of your arm." As he talked he as he signaled her to stand and made the needed length adjustment. "I think you'll find this much easier on you. I had planned for you to try two, but now I'll need to keep one for myself."

"It wasn't the climbing that was so bad with Dalton, it was coming down. I felt that at any moment my knees would give out. I couldn't lock them for control like I did going up"

"I have some ideas about that, too." He said smiling, but didn't elaborate.

They headed toward one of the rocky faces near where they had entered the bowl-like valley. He signaled her through a narrow cleft of rock and a trail appeared. She noticed two ropes dangling from the towering top of the cliff, but continued on at his urging. He watched her closely as they slowly ascended, each supported by their cane. Whenever she tired and her steps began to slightly shuffle, he would call a halt. He reminded her it was important to take frequent rests, before she got too tired. If she didn't over extend herself, she could keep going for a long time. They finally came to a somewhat wider spot in the trail. Beyond that spot the trail turned abruptly around the rock face. But that wasn't what caused Ann's intake of breath. The cliff on her right was still overshadowing, but on the left side of the trail dropped sharply away. It was a long way down!

Ben urged her away from the edge toward the rock face. He cleared a spot for them to sit comfortably and then sat with his back against the wall. He pulled her gently down and close against his side. "We'll take a longer rest here," he said. He quieted her question with a kiss, leaned back and tucked her head against his shoulder. Soon her steady breathing told him she was asleep. He looked at her and felt a rush of tenderness. Ben pulled her more tightly to him and was rewarded with her arms slipping unconsciously around his chest. Goodbye Angie, he thought. I've clung to my bitter feelings about you for too many years. My misreading of you and your wants has kept me from trusting a woman for way too long. I had abandoned the hope that this would ever happen, but I love this woman.

When Ann awoke, Ben opened his pack and removed a rope. He took each of the collapsing canes, folded and tucked them into the pack. "You're not going to need this but I think it will give you more confidence," he said, tying the rope firmly around her waist. I'll keep a light tension on it and it will stabilize you. I'll go first this time. Put one foot in front of the other, just look at your feet, not down!" He said this quickly and then led off around the corner.

She followed for only a few steps. What she saw made her stomach turn flops. The nice wide trail they had been following stopped for a gap of about ten feet. Ben was starting across the narrow section now. Luckily the bluff's face sloped away on his right, so there was plenty of room for his hips and shoulders. There was a rope stretched tightly to his left held by a sturdy looking rock projection on this side and some huge boulders on the far side. The line was undoubtedly some protection from a fall down the precipice but it seemed worth not much more than a thread to her frightened mind. The path itself was almost non-existent. She immediately saw what he meant about one foot in front of the other. That was all there was space for, since the trail was only about 6 inches wide.

Despite favoring his foot, Ben was across in a few seconds but it seemed forever.

"Now, it's your turn," he called, but she held back.

"I can't. I flunk the walking heel to toe test every time I go to the Doctor. I can't keep my balance doing that."

"This is different. Don't go heel to toe. Take longer strides. It's only about four or five steps. Stretch your left hand out and touch the rope. Don't lean on it unless you have to. I'll be holding your waist rope, too." He noticed her continuing hesitation and took a step back toward her. "If I carry you across, it will be dangerous. But, I hope I don't need to. Do it! Now!"

His gaze seemed to will her forward. She moved. Each step was agony but she made it across without a problem. As she reached safety on the widened trail, he gathered her in his arms. "I knew you could."

Despite his words, he was clinging to her. She felt a shiver go through him. She pulled back a little and looked into his eyes. What she saw there dropped the last of the protective shell around her heart. She hadn't even known she was holding anything back. The feeling flooded her suddenly. I want to be close to this man, so close I could crawl right into his skin. Her arms encircled his neck and pulled him to her lips.

When they finally had their fill of each other, Ben brought out their canes and they continued the short walk to the top. He led her forward to the most breath-taking view she could imagine. To the north Mt. Rainier pushed its glistening peak skyward. To the South was something she had never seen, except in pictures. She and Em had talked several times about taking a ride down that way but hadn't made it yet.

The photographs and videos she'd seen didn't begin to do the mountain justice. Mount Saint Helens' devastated crater was almost overpowering. The devastation was almost more than the mind come grasp.

She stood there gazing in awe for several minutes, drinking in the spectacle. She hugged Ben. He was right. It was worth the effort. Then he stepped away, pulled a light blanket from his pack and spread it about five feet back from the edge. "You aren't tired are you, Ann?"

"No. I just had a nap, remember? I feel great."

"Good." He stepped near her, reached for her hand and lifted it to the front of his shirt. He put her fingers tightly around the zipper tab and then pulled down.

"You are insatiable." She teased him. He just smiled, tugged again on her hand, and he waited as she undressed him. When she had finished she looked at him, expecting him to do the same for her, but he shook his head no. As she undressed, he just crossed his arms and observed. But she knew the sight was appreciated as she watched his desire grow. There was no doubt how she affected him. It made her tingle from head to toe.

Ben sat down with his back to the cliff, legs out in front of him. At his urging she knelt over his legs. His mouth quickly found her breast, he pulled her forward onto his hardened member. She was ready.

Ben lay back. The breeze from the cliff side blew over her dampened breasts caressing her gently. "Today you're in charge, ma'am." He said. Then he goaded her with his hips to move. She did, shyly at first, but with growing desire. Seeing him just lay there his hands folded on his chest watching her, she realized she was expected to do all the initiating. She was in total control. It was intoxicating. Soon she felt the need of his involvement with what was happening to her. She cautiously reached for his hands and brought them to her breasts. He gave her a smile and responded just as tenuously, teasing her nipples lightly. That wasn't enough and Ann pulled his hands firmly against the hardening mounds. She was becoming more aroused and her caution flew away. She pushed one of his hands downward and pressed it to her.

Screeech! She stiffened at the screams; her eyes flew open and searched for the source. An eagle passed closely in front of them, with wings larger than she had ever imagined. She felt as if she soared with him, as she sensed a building fire.

Suddenly her muscles tired. Please!—Not now, her mind begged. But he sensed it, too. His hands grasped her hips and his powerful help gave the added strength to bring them to release.

She collapsed forward onto his chest. Now she knew why men always fell asleep. After a brief respite, she started chuckling. "So, am I supposed to amend my autobiography to add consummation in an eagle's nest?"

His grin matched hers. "Not bad. You do have a little imagination in you, if you try."

She snuggled back to his chest still smiling. Suddenly she sat back up. "This scene is just too planned. Have you done this here before?"

"One other woman, I thought about bringing here 20 years ago. Back then both mountains were whole. I had a notion they represented the two of us. In my youth, I loved symbolism. Well, it didn't happen. Now, look at St. Helens. She's slightly wounded but still majestic. She's still a worthy partner for Rainier. They make an impregnable pair. You could find some symbolism in that, too. But the real answer to your question is; only in my dreams, and I have to tell you the reality is better."

"You do have the most exotic dreams." She said lying back down.

"I do, and I have more. One I like involves mud."

"No way! How could you imagine such a thing?"

He laughed as he pulled the blanket around them. "I know you don't fantasize. It's just a waste of precious time when you could be making money, driving ahead to build your security, but just let that thought run around in the back of your mind. Mud." He continued laughing quietly to himself. Against her will the idea did stay with her and the beginning of a little daydream followed her as she napped on his chest.

Later, he pulled a light lunch from his pack. Ben told her he felt it would be better not to have too much on her stomach on the trip down. She didn't really understand why, but enjoyed the snack. After a while she brought to his attention the beautiful black clouds forming off to their right. As she did, a spectacular bolt of lightening streaked toward the hills.

"Ben! We don't want to be on the highest point around if that storm moves this way."

He bounded up. They quickly folded the canes, picked up the remnants of lunch and the blanket and stored them in the pack. Then he took her hand, but instead of heading for the trailhead, he moved along to top of the bluff into the sparse trees. There was no trail but he led her carefully over the obstacles. Finally he turned back toward the edge. There were two huge trees with some rigging around them from which ropes led over the side of the cliff.

He let her drink it in. Then he told her he had a terrible fear of heights. He decided to do something about it and joined the Mountaineers. He took classes, climbed a few minor peaks and culminated with Mt. Rainier. He'd also done a little rock climbing. He didn't like most of it, but rappelling back down he found exhilarating. This is where he practiced and he'd added a second rope for her. "I planned to spend a little more time getting you ready for this, but the fat's in the fire now. We need to get down." He explained that she could be in double harness with him or, as he hoped, she could go on her own. He would coach her through the techniques and stay just a few feet below her. "I never would have suggested it, but it's really easy on your legs and knees. I know that's important to you." He teased. He proceeded with the coaching and fit the harness. She still held back. He urged her. "You can do anything you need to. This is just one more obstacle. You can make it past this one, too." She moved cautiously toward the edge.

He backed over first and coached her down. He stayed just a few feet ahead of her and encouraged her all the way. When she reached the bottom, she felt a rush of accomplishment. "I knew you could." He told her.

"I'm glad you were sure, I certainly wasn't. I can't even remember much about the trip down. I just did it without thinking."

"That's the point. I don't believe there's anyone I'd rather be with in a crisis. No fuss, just resolve and no talk. You know how I like keeping the talk to a minimum." He hugged her until she thought her ribs would give way. "Now we'd better get back to the house before the rain catches us." They held each other as they walked back to the cabin.

CHAPTER 12

The rest of the day Ben suggested that they should just relax but for him this meant a lot of little maintenance duties. As they worked at the chores together, Ann saw how comfortable they had become in the last few months. They operated well as a team. Often she sensed what he would do next and had the right tool ready or was at the other end of something that needed to be held in place. When this happened he beamed at her like a proud father over a child.

Whenever they rested, they fell into conversation easily. But today their talks edged toward what the future might hold for them.

"I think," Ben mentioned, "you'll find salaries in Seattle a little lower than you're used to, but the cost of living should drop proportionally." After giving her a minute to think that over, he went on. "Even so, if you lived there during the week and commuted here, you'll probably use nearly half your net income. What you'll soon see is that what's left will be above the take home of most people around here. Still, when you live on land that's paid for, have a garden, bake, hunt and do some canning; the cost of living just isn't that high. Folks here are happy with their life style. It's relaxed, but it's a good one." He didn't wait for a reply but moved off and left her to think about that.

Later he headed back to the subject. "After living in the urban setting for so many years, there's probably a lot you would miss. I understand that you wouldn't be content to live here."

"I don't think you do. I like the slower pace. I love the people and the country, except for the rain. I just need to earn a living. If I knew I could do that here, I would. But this area is not booming with new work. I've read the unemployment stats. Because of the logging cut back, this isn't a healthy economy. Besides there is nothing vaguely close to clothing design here."

"You're right. I was waffling around a bit and I said that very poorly. Let me try again. I want you in my life. No matter how unconventional the arrangement may seem to other people. I know you need to go to Seattle for work. I couldn't ever live there. I don't go to A. A. meetings anymore. This place gives me the peace I need to stay sober. If you lived in Seattle, I would come and see you sometimes. I would be here every weekend if you came down. I know there are places in this world you probably want to go. I would not join you. I don't have any interest in foreign travel but I would never want you to forgo anything."

"I'm not sure how to answer that. It seems you are moving us pretty fast."

"Don't answer it. Think about it. It's not fast for me because I've thought of little else since the first few weeks you were here. I've tried to decide how to approach you. I didn't want to scare you off—ruin what fun we've had with each other. I knew my time was almost up before you left for Seattle and found someone else. I knew I had to get you to look at me as more than a horse wrangler on your personal dude ranch."

"Hey. I never said that!"

"You didn't have to. I could tell you felt that it was beneath your station to show any interest in the ranch hand. There were days I sensed that you might be wavering, but I wasn't sure."

Ann laughed as she thought back realistically over the last few months. "I guess you had me pegged! I felt a tension between us, even that first day. I shut it down with almost those same words. 'What would Aunt Em think...the ranch hand.' It seemed too much like a dime novel. There have been times since then when I felt a tug but..."

"Let's see...bent nose, old man, going nowhere, stealing from old ladies, horse crazy, no money...That kind of sum it up?"

"Not consciously, but maybe, sort of. How did you get that little crook in your nose, falling off a horse?"

"No. Barroom brawls and a little boxing. Don't try and change the subject. The money thing we'll ignore, I don't want any woman making up her mind about me based on that. Besides, you can see that I support my stock and myself just fine. It doesn't bother me, if it won't bother you when you out earn me many times over."

"That's no big deal. I think it could be fun to have a kept man. I think the broken nose adds a little character."

"We beat the 'old' thing around a little. You fighting the M.S. and me being older ought to put us about even in what we're willing to take on. The only issue that leaves is that M.S. doesn't lower life expectancy; it just impacts life style. So that means if you hooked up with me, you would probably spend your last years alone. Especially with all the drinking and pounding I've taken with that rodeo craziness. Hard to say if I'll have much longevity."

"Whoa! We haven't gotten past tomorrow and you're already planning a lifetime. But just for the sake of discussion, as it stands now, I'll be spending my foreseeable future alone—including my last years—so that's not an issue."

"What is an issue?"

"I don't know. Maybe I'm a little concerned about breaking this change to Em. What will she think? I still have the M.S. on my mind, too. Without knowing what's ahead, how can you commit yourself? I wouldn't if I had any way out. I want to believe this is real, but I think

I need time to breathe—to think—not just jump with my emotions in a whirl."

"There's the practical business woman. That's fair. I've got no problem with one day at a time. That is my way of living. For today and tonight then, you'll stay?"

Ann nodded.

They savored the evening in the valley, with the rough and cragged cliffs closing them tightly in but also forming a wall against the rest of the world. They continued to revel at their strengthening bond.

The next day they reluctantly got ready to go back to face the world. Ann told Ben she wanted to do a little on her job search before Em returned. Ben brought out another shirt. This one was brand new, not even out of the package yet. He started to tell her that she was welcome to continue on as she was, but she stopped him with a fierce look. They both knew she would never be content to live off him and her aunt. "Yes. Ma'am," he acquiesced.

When they had things packed up, he told her he would bring the horses back the next day and led the way on a well worn path toward the dip in the cliffs where the creek flowed in. She remembered from the drawing, and from Bronco's visit that there was another way out and this was it. A series of small falls brought the creek in over the bluff. Beside it she saw a flight of steep stairs cut into the rock with no handrail. There was a large steel basket with heavy cable extending to the top of the bluff. A crane-like arm supported the line. Ben put their things in the basket.

"You can try the stairs or ride in the basket. The winch is plenty strong enough to handle you, this is how I got all the materials for the house down here. It's designed to handle a ton. It's electric," he said as he pulled the controls out of their protected niche in the cliff face, "and it's a fast trip up."

"I'd better go with the basket. But, how do you get power to this thing?"

"You'll see when we get up there."

As the basket cleared the top edge of the valley, she felt she had stepped forward a century from the pastoral setting in the valley. There was a large blue sheet metal building, a tall pole supporting a mercury vapor yard light, and a cyclone fence surrounding the area. Above them on one side was something that looked like a small satellite dish.

Ben started explaining what she was looking at. "The building I put up to protect all of Henry's logging equipment. It's big enough to handle the truck with or without the trailer stacked up. All the other equipment and the trailer to haul it just fit in around that. I keep my pick-up in there, too. The cyclone fence gives me some privacy protection. This is the only publicly accessible entrance into my hideaway. That's the county road you can see just beyond the gate. Luckily the height of the surrounding hills keeps the sound of traffic out of the valley. Now that dish you were looking at is a little something I worked out with the phone company. The telephone does come in handy. On the other hand, I couldn't fathom telephone lines and poles coming across the open space in the valley. Digging a trench on the rocky valley floor didn't seem reasonable, so I use this little radio system and it does the trick."

She marveled again at his capacity to deal with the minute details it took to make everything about this valley special. She asked him how he kept track of everything. "Lists, of course," he replied. "I'll show you my collection sometime. I keep them in sets. For example: maintenance to do's. Those are kind of organized by season then for the homestead vs. the valley. But my favorites are the ideas for new additions. There are lots of possibilities. I expect we'll be working on those and adding to them for the rest of our lives." Ben favored Ann with a crooked little grin as he gave her a quick hug.

Hand in hand they went into the building, got out the pick-up and drove to the M bar M. They parked at his usual place by the barn and walked slowly to the house, holding each other close. It was a real surprise when Em greeted them as they came through the door.

"Your Blazer's not out front!", burst out Ann.

"Hal took it to town, he'll be back in a while." She ignored Ann's shocked look. Ben saw Em's eyes shift to him when she recognized the shirt Ann was wearing. It was the one Em had given him for him for his birthday. She'd been needling him because she hadn't seen him wear it. Ann was still too confused to notice when Ben smiled and shrugged.

"Ann," Em continued, "I'm glad you made it back early, too. I assume you two talked about the logging." They both nodded. "Good. Ann, there's an urgent message from Pam Rausch, you'd better call her right away."

Ann told her she'd already called and gave her the good news.

Em hugged her in congratulations. Ben pointed out, a little smugly Ann thought, that she didn't need to hunt for work in Seattle immediately. Looked like her hands would be full here for a while.

"That's great, but first I have a little bone to pick with you Ben. You stinker, Hal took me to the motor home factory in Oregon. That was quite a surprise!" She hugged him, too. "We picked one out, but have to go back for it. They're adding a tow bar and a few other extras. We resolved as long as we're going first class might as well be in for a pound. We also decided to give our arthritis some relief from the wet winter. Thought we'd join the snowbird rush and head to Arizona for a while this winter. Ann, someone needs to be familiar with my work." As she talked, she led them into her bedroom and rolled up the top on the large desk.

Ann was startled. Much of the space was taken up with a computer system. Em sat down and brought up the file manager, accompanied by commentary on how she filed. "Here's how I have the books set up for The Homestead. I also like to keep the forms on hand that I think we might need. I download some of them from the Internet." She reached for a little book. "Here's where I keep all the

URL's for the sites Ben needs me to access for data. It's more than government agencies; I watch beef prices, and the stock market. You can review these later and see what I mean. These folders here are things I print to study a little more when I get time."

The file folders were, Ann noticed, held in a stand so each title was clearly visible. Included among them was one on M. S., and another labeled Motor Homes.

"Em, you're wonderfully organized and sure have all the jargon down." Ann laughed. "When do you find time to do this?"

"I know you think we go to bed pretty early around here, but I'm actually kind of a night owl. I do a little each evening. Originally I thought I'd just use this for email to keep in contact with grand-nieces and nephews. Unlike Henry's family, on my side, we're a pretty big gang. Kids today don't use stationary, so to hear from them; I have keep up with the times. Then, Ben and I went partners. I wanted to do something to earn the money he given me, since he bought the place years ago. He hates the computer, so it seemed like a natural."

Ann spun on Ben. "Owns the whole place?"

Em went on before he could answer. "He's so stubborn about that. He insists we call it a partnership and keep the land title between us. He says it upholds my standing in the community. That's rubbish! Nobody cares one way or the other."

"So, why," Ann asked him, "do you do it?"

"Well, I just figured it would keep women from running after me for my money. It's has worked well. I try to stick with what works."

Both the women ignored his chuckles and let his little tease pass.

Em continued. "I did the books for Henry so it was a natural to do ours, too. After Ben paid off the mortgage, I told him he should just own all the land, since I would have lost it. But he had the timber cruised and valued and I realized I hadn't mortgaged it for anywhere near its real market value. So we compromised. Ben has title but is giving me a set amount each month for the rest of my life. In return I do the paperwork, you know, taxes or whatever. You may not be a bookkeeper but I think I have things set up here so you can just follow."

Ann couldn't believe that he had told her all about his stock market holdings and forgot to mention this. What was it Em called him? Stinker—that fit!

Ben looked a little sheepish. "Well I guess really I wanted to keep it quiet for Em. Although she keeps insisting otherwise, I think it does make a difference. There's a certain pride to owning your own place. As far as I'm concerned, it's still hers regardless what the title says. Then, too, Bronco always goes on about how he can't stand the big boys, I didn't want to have him fretting about the inequality in our financial standing. I just found out yesterday, it doesn't matter to Bronco either."

Ann could see that Ben felt deeply about this. He didn't like to talk about his own generosity to Em any more than his concern for Bronco or even Fiero. Ann shifted the topic to give him a way out. She told them she'd like to check her email, since the computer system was handy. Some of her Chicago friends were probably wondering what had happened to her. She had a guilty thought that she'd better put Ed Lorence on her list of people to call. Now that she was firmly settled in Washington and finding work in Seattle, she needed to let him know. She logged-on to her electronic mail system. There were many messages waiting, most of them from Ed. But she started with the oldest one from her friend and coworker, Amy.

The message said that Ed was being something of a jerk. He had promoted Larry Waznik (a manager with whom Ann rarely agreed) to Ann's position only two days after she left. Ed said it was temporary, but Larry wasted no time moving into her office. Ann felt a vicious twist in her insides as she read. Even though she was quitting, to see that she wouldn't be missed was a blow to her ego.

She skipped down to another message from Amy sent only a week ago. It said that Ed was frantic. Larry was not working out at all. Ed was trying everything to figure out how to get in touch with Ann. He wanted her to come back early from her leave.

Ben was standing close behind her reading over her shoulder. He moved his hand possessively to caress her neck when he read that. They both failed to see the speculative look on Em's face as she watched them.

Ann went back to the first message from Ed. It had been sent about two weeks after she left.

'Hope you're doing well. Give us a call sometime.'

It wasn't even signed. The next message was about a month later.

'Haven't heard from you. A lot of us here are interested in how things are going. Let us know where we can contact you.'

Again, it was not signed. Ann didn't like the feeling that gave her. She always signed her messages, because it made them more personal. The bunch of us reference made a pretty firm statement, too. The message was not personal. Ed's notes came with more frequency after that, but didn't add much new. The last one had come yesterday. It was the first one that used the word 'I'.

ॐ

'I need to know where I can contact you. You've always been a key to our success. I've learned in the last few months just how valuable you are. I realize that I owe you a raise. I know I can make it worth your while to stay with us, rather than looking around the industry.

I miss you, Ann. I need you here beside me.

With Love,

Ed'

Ann couldn't believe that he was desperate enough to play that hand! What dishonesty to only say those things when her replacement got himself in over his head. She was angry, through and through. Any twinge of guilt she felt about not going back was erased. She selected REPLY and typed quickly.

∽

'Sorry for the short notice. I quit. It's not negotiable.'

She hit SEND before she could change her mind and logged off.

Seeing she was done, Em jumped in. "Now you two get out of here. I need to clean up the mess I made dragging all this stuff out. I'll catch up with you in a minute."

When they reached the main room, Ben took her hand and led her toward the living area. She immediately noted a new addition. The chair, you might call it, hung from a twisted wire rope. She looked up and saw the cable went through a pulley hooked to the swiveling arm on the main log beam. The chair itself was constructed of steel or aluminum with wood added, maybe to make it fit in better with the decor. The seat was covered in a tapestry that coordinated with Em's furnishings. Ben walked over and sat in the chair pulling her into his lap.

"Safety first." He said as he retrieved a belt out of a little compartment and fastened it across them. Out of a compartment in the arm rest Ben retrieved a remote like the one that controlled the metal basket out of the valley. He touched it and they rose slowly to the loft. There he showed her the gate that had been made in the railing and demonstrated how to easily open the latch and swing the chair onto the loft.

"How did you get this done?" She asked.

"Well, I've been planning it ever since the night we had that dinner with Dalton and Hal. I saw you come down those stairs, remember? I decided I'd better get working on a better arrangement. I designed it and ordered the stuff, but with the logging and all, I just didn't get it installed. So when I talked to Bronco the other day, I had him get some men up here to have it ready for you. You like it?"

"Yes, but I like you better. I've never known anyone as thought-ful."

"I want more than to be liked." He told her and followed it with an ardent kiss. "I know you've been out to the old cabin. One of the things I love about The Homestead, for you, is that you can go most anywhere without walking. I fixed that old cedar seat but I've always gone there alone. The only other person I could ever share that with is a special woman who would sit there in my arms. I want to be there with you, Ann. The woman I love."

"It's all happening so fast, but I..."

"Hey, you two get down here." Em yelled.

They jumped like two kids with their hands caught in the cookie jar. Their eyes still held. He knew what she was about to say. They both nodded and then burst out laughing at their clearly communi-cated mutual feelings.

"Yes. Ma'am," Ben called back. They hurried to the winch-chair, but Ann stopped Ben before they stepped in. "It's nice to hear it directly sometimes", she said seriously. "I love you, Ben."

"I love you, too, Kawheelah", he told her sealing it with a quick hug. Any thoughts of continuing their embrace was cut short by the sobering sound of Em's tapping foot. They hurriedly strapped back in the chair and ran the winch down.

Em watched them snuggled in the chair. Ben's arm was around Ann possessively. Their eyes never left each other and they both looked like they'd swallowed a canary! Their smiles seemed perma-nently affixed.

"So," she said when they alit, "I see you've worked out your differ-ences." She grinned mischievously. "I'd just about given up on you two. I've believed you'd fit for years. First, I couldn't convince Ann to come out here and there was no sense in even suggesting that Ben go to Chicago! Then when she finally agrees, he," she pointed an accus-ing finger, "grows that infernal beard and starts dressing like a bum." Ben flushed. "I thought for a while my Dalton, jealousy gambit was going to backfire. Then when that worked out," Em went on. "Ann calls in the cavalry to save me from a crook! I just about had heart failure over that. That's when I gave up."

Their surprise turned to anger as they realized they had been out maneuvered. "Em! How could you?" Ann cried. Ben just shook his head, he'd been fighting Em over fixing him up for years.

"Oh. Get those outraged looks off your faces!" Em chided them. "I was right, wasn't I?"

When they glanced at each other, both puffed up over something they were deliriously happy about, their anger turned to laughter.

"So now that you've come to your senses and stopped fighting the inevitable, does this mean there will be a double wedding next month?"

Ben pulled Ann close against him. "Sounds right to me. How about it?"

It certainly wasn't the proposal she'd always dreamed of! She looked up into his rugged face. With that slightly crooked nose, beard and some wrinkles from age and the sun; he wasn't the dashing Prince Charming she'd envisioned. Still, this felt right. She could have a good life with this man. "Yes." She said simply and was promptly crushed in his arms.

"How about a double honeymoon, too?"

"Oh. No." Ann quickly told her. "Ben has made it clear that traveling isn't for him."

"Really? Well, I'm not sure when it starts. We might have to defer our trip a little, but what I have in mind is snowmobiling in the Grand Tetons."

"You know. I've always wanted to do that." Ben commented.

Em adopted a fatuous look. "You see dear," she told Ann, "when he says no travel, he just means being locked up on a cruise ship or going to anywhere with lots of people. With a little imagination, you can find lots of places where he'll gladly go."

Ann looked at Ben with a question in her eyes and caught a sheepish look, before he captured her in another embrace.

"Good, then it's settled." Em broke in. "Now you two can knock it
off. There's plenty of time for <u>that</u>. There's not much time for all the
planning. Ann and I will start on that right now. You," she said
pointing at Ben, "better get down to the barn. Bronco has a number
of issues for you."

"Yes. Ma'am," he said. Grinning from ear to ear, he headed out the
door.

Epilogue

The dual wedding was the social event of the season in Morton. Ann designed and sewed wedding gowns for herself and Em. Since both women were slender, the straight-lines of the simple floor length antique satin gowns were stunning. Ann cleverly made each dress slightly unique with lace touches to emphasize the best features of each. Hal and Em went to Arizona in their new motor home for most of the cold wet winter season

The foursome waited for the best snow conditions in March to have a deferred official honeymoon near Jackson Hole, Wyoming. It was spectacular in every way. With a guide to help them through the rough spots they thoroughly enjoyed their first experience with snowmobiles.

Em and Hal spend a lot of time on the road in their new motor home. Ann has her hands full keeping up with everything Em assigns her while they're gone. Ann also has her own portfolio to watch. She took the money planned for a condo unit and invested it in the stock market. The income from that takes care of her medical expenses. Her art and advertising income provides for extras that keep her comfortably independent.

Ann never did go on to Seattle, except for an occasional 'meet the artist' promotional event. Somehow, her original plans for a move to the city disappeared in the whirl of her new life with Ben and total involvement in a real community.

Bronco's part-time work has expanded as Ann and Ben have left to explore parts of Alaska and Montana. They have a trip to British Columbia scheduled with Em and Hal next spring.

Dalton's life is proceeding according to plan. He married a 25-year-old socialite really succeeded in having two plus children, a boy and twin girls. He helped Ben finalize the legalities of his old-growth legacy.

Ann has had a few nasty M.S. episodes. When that happens, Ben's inventive mind and engineering skills are put to the test, and have resulted in a number of new conveniences at the cabin. Their commitment to each other has kept their relationship strong and growing as the years have passed.

Ann hasn't learned what Ben's fantasy about mud is—yet!